"You Wanted A Ride, Didn't You?"

Raven handed her his spare helmet and climbed onto his motorcycle. After she buckled it on, she just stood there, as if she were contemplating the enormity of what she was doing.

"So—get on. Ever ridden one of these before?" he asked as she warily climbed on behind him.

"My mother always told me not to," came her warm, breathy voice against his ear.

"And you were a good girl who did everything Mama said?"

"Oh, no. I'm not sure I've ever followed a single piece of advice she gave me," she admitted guiltily.

His kind of girl. "Hang on to me—tight."

****

Something Wild . . . Take a walk on the *wild* side with Ann Major's sizzling stories featuring Honey, Midnight . . . and Innocence!

Dear Reader,

You can tell from the presence of some *very* handsome hunks on the covers that something special is going on for Valentine's Day here at Silhouette Desire! That "something" is a group of guys we call "Bachelor Boys"... you know, those men who think they'll never get "caught" by a woman—until they do! They're our very special Valentine's Day gift to you.

The lineup is pretty spectacular: a *Man of the Month* by Ann Major, and five other fabulous books by Raye Morgan, Peggy Moreland, Karen Leabo, Audra Adams and a *brand-new* to Silhouette author, Susan Carroll. You won't be able to pick up just one! So, you'll have to buy all six of these delectable, sexy stories.

Next month, we have even more fun in store: a *Man of the Month* from the sizzling pen of Jackie Merritt, a delicious story by Joan Johnston, and four more wonderful Desire love stories.

So read... and enjoy... as these single guys end up *happily* tamed by the women of their dreams.

Until next month,

Lucia Macro
Senior Editor

Please address questions and book requests to:
Reader Service
U.S.: P.O. Box 1325, Buffalo, NY 14269
Canadian: P.O. Box 1050, Niagara Falls, Ont. L2E 7G7

ANN
MAJOR
WILD INNOCENCE

SILHOUETTE *Desire*®
Published by Silhouette Books
America's Publisher of Contemporary Romance

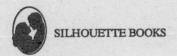

SILHOUETTE BOOKS

ISBN 0-373-05835-7

WILD INNOCENCE

This edition published by arrangement with Harlequin Enterprises B. V.

® and TM are trademarks of Harlequin Enterprises B. V., used under
license. Trademarks indicated with ® are registered in the United States
Patent and Trademark Office, the Canadian Trade Marks Office and in
other countries.

Printed in U.S.A.

Books by Ann Major

ANN MAJOR

is not only a successful author, but she also manages a business and runs a busy household with three children. She lists traveling and playing the piano among her many interests—her favorite composer, quite naturally, is the romantic Chopin.

One

A fierce, brittle tension swept C block, giving even the most hardened big-timers of that Texas prison a malevolent rush of exhilaration.

Word was out. There was going to be a hit. Raven Wyatt—or White, as the men believed his name to be—was going to die. Today.

And it would be a real pleasure to watch that cocky bastard go down.

Raven had seen men die here. He'd seen them crawl and beg before being hacked to pieces, and his fear consumed every part of him. It was devouring him from the inside and producing a nausea so fierce it almost took his breath away. His absolute terror amazed him, because until today he'd thought anything, even his own death, was preferable to being warehoused in this cage of human refuse for the rest of his life for a crime he hadn't committed.

Now he knew he was scared of dying. He was scared of groveling and disgracing himself as a coward.

Because that's what they wanted.

Not that Raven looked afraid as he shuffled down the crowded, unguarded *C*-wing hallway jammed with fifty other prisoners—any one of whom could be his murderer. Except for being taller, he didn't look much different from the other white-clad men. His broad shoulders were hunched like theirs. His green eyes were flat and zombie-like from what everyone assumed was his most recent megadose of Thorazine. Rumor was it had taken three guards to hold him down for the injection. Which was good, those plotting his death agreed. It would make him easier to kill.

Despite the clammy chill in the dank hallway, Raven was sweating profusely. How the snitch had laughed when he'd gloatingly informed Raven that Snake and the others were going to cut him down and gut him like a steer in a slaughterhouse.

Suddenly out of nowhere Snake struck—rattler fast.

Prisoners stampeded in panic to get out of his way and Raven found himself alone in that shadowy hallway, cut off from the guards and any help by the locked crash gate behind him.

There were four of them—treacherous killers every one. The huge brutes were so sure of themselves, they didn't even spread out, but came toward him in a single mass. Death was to be a sixteen-inch hand-tooled shank gleaming in Snake's dark hand, which suddenly lashed out at Raven's throat.

Raven jumped aside, but not fast enough. The jagged tip had slashed his shirt and hit his collarbone before he lunged back against the bars. Arredo caught him off balance and drove a savage knee into his groin. In a haze of pain, Raven doubled over as one of the other thugs got behind him and used a hand to force his head back so the next knife thrust would finish him.

Blindly, futilely Raven fought as they wrestled him to the floor. He screamed and rolled, and the shank missed his throat again, plunging into his shoulder this time. In the scuffle Snake's hand slipped, and he fell, cursing. Then Raven grabbed the jutting hilt and ripped the knife out of his own flesh, stabbing wildly at Snake, then at the rest of them, hitting two of them, as they scrambled to get away from him. He fought them like a maddened beast for an endless, hellish eternity, until they were gone and he was alone, lying prostrate on the floor, the only sound that from his lungs rasping for air.

He heard shouts, running feet.

"Fight!"

Keys clinked, and through a haze of blood, he saw half a dozen boots in blue uniforms rushing toward him.

The fight was over, or the cowards wouldn't have come.

Too weak to get up, Raven realized he was lying beside a lifeless body. He recognized the rattler tattooed on the limp brown hand. One of the new boots, as guards were called, pressed thick towels to Raven's throat and shoulder to staunch the flow of blood.

But it was too late. Raven could feel the sticky wetness pooling around him as he began to sink into an all-engulfing, eternal blackness.

Someone hurried toward him with a gurney.

No doubt to haul his corpse to the morgue.

The blackness grew colder; the boot's young face blurred. And suddenly Raven was in a chilling white mist, and it was *her* face that he saw, the terrible, but oh-so-lovely features that had haunted him every day and every night since he'd seen her. For although he hadn't known it at the time, she had been the beginning of this nightmare.

How prim and proper she looked in his mind's eye, with her silk blouse buttoned demurely all the way up to her neck. With her red hair caught up in that tight, little bun on top of her head. With that tense expression and vulnerable look that told a man she was all tied up in knots.

And suddenly the wind was blowing and she was shaking her head and her flaming hair was spilling free like loose clouds of fire all about her shoulders. Her fingers were unclasping the buttons, one by one, and she was pushing her blouse down to her waist. Her expression changed, and instead of an innocent, she was a wanton.

Then she leaned toward him and branded him with the hottest kisses he had ever known. He was sinking into bed with her. They were both naked, and she was kissing him everywhere and laughing as their lips and bodies melted together, laughing, still, as she began to writhe.

It wasn't a dream.

It was a memory from that other lifetime before prison.

He'd felt he'd been alone all his life, till he'd met her. He hadn't known then that she was the devil's own, who with her lies had lured him to his doom and cast him into hell as surely as some siren from some ancient mythic tale.

He had been betrayed before—terribly, when he'd been little more than a boy by his own father, Hunter Wyatt, and Astella, the woman he had thought he'd loved—but not nearly so terribly as by this redheaded witch. Because of her, Pam was dead and he was in prison.

His pulse flickered as more of his lifeblood seeped from his wounds.

He was dying.

Maybe it was for the best.

Then he saw *her* face. And again he realized that he didn't want to die.

With a fierce, indomitable will he struggled against death just as bitterly as he had when he'd fought Snake.

He *had* to survive. If it was the last thing he ever did, he had to find out who she was and why she'd done what she'd done. He would get out of this hellhole—and make her pay.

The coldness grew more profound, and as it did his crazed brain seemed to slow. But nothing dimmed the image of her beautiful face. It was still there, taunting him.

If he was really going to die, he shouldn't think of her. He should remember San Francisco, the home of his youth. He should remember his mother or his younger sister, Honey, but all he recalled of his brief childhood in that mansion overlooking the hills and bay was bitter loneliness and the terrible feeling that he hadn't mattered to anyone.

He saw a little boy taking refuge from his angry father behind a huge canvas. Raven Wyatt cowered as he watched his famous mother paint with long passionate strokes and vivid splashes of color. More than anything Raven had wanted his mother to feel such passion for him. He longed for her to take him in her arms, to love him, to shield him from his dictatorial father's wrath—just once. But Raven had known that if he had come out from behind the huge canvas and begged for her love she would have screamed at him and banished him, because the only thing that mattered to her was her art. Her paintings were her real children, and when she wasn't painting she left the house and partied, preferring the company of chic, glamorous strangers to her children.

Raven remembered curling up at the foot of her bed, waiting like a faithful dog for her to return from her late night parties, hoping for a glimpse of her when she came in, hoping at least to awaken and find her sleeping. Then she had died, and he'd been left with a father who hated him.

No, it was sweeter to forget San Francisco, as he had done for years, and to remember the May afternoon two summers ago, when he'd met the witch.

Raven's eyelids fluttered. His lips moved as he gasped the only name he knew to call her by.

And because the young boot thought the gray-faced convict was dying, and significance is placed upon the last utterance of any man, he leaned closer to catch the strangled syllables wrenched from that torn throat with such hideous effort.

"Sweet Hitchhiker."

Raven's lips stopped moving, and he lapsed into the black, fevered world of nightmare.

Two

Raven's cold, bleeding body lay inert on a hard cot in the prison infirmary, while his mind whirled backward in time to the woman who had been at the beginning of his nightmare.

One minute Raven had been racing his huge motorcycle through misting rain, down that desolate Texas hill-country road away from Pam's house, as if a dozen demons were chasing him.

In the next he was slowing his bike as he neared the slick curve that came before the low water bridge at Scud's Crossing, and a *hitchhiker* had materialized on the shoulder of the narrow road, seeming to take shape as if by magic, as if she were some enchanted creature conceived of mist and fog.

She was a slim, dazzling figure in white with shimmery, fiery hair pulled up in a strange, little knot at the top of her head. With a hesitant gesture that told him she was new at this sport, she held up her hand and cocked her thumb at him.

Raven should have known better than to pick up a hitchhiker in such a lonely place. Thirty-seven was old enough to know that evil often can come in any guise. But one does not expect evil to be standing beside the road above the rippling green Blanco River on a soft spring day in the form of a beguiling woman with huge, innocent eyes. And in those days, fear was almost an unknown emotion to him.

He would learn that later.

Because of her.

In prison.

Besides, when he'd run from San Francisco, he'd gotten to Texas by hitching a ride with his now-dearest friend and mentor, Frank Clark.

Besides, the girl looked so helpless and terrified in that vaporous swirl of ground fog coming off the river and swirling around the limestone cliffs and springtime flowers. It had seemed uncanny that she should appear, a week to the day, in the exact spot where the road dipped and curved before the bridge, the exact spot Frank Clark had died in a head-on collision with the town's drunk, Sam Lescuer. Especially since Raven had intended to stop there anyway—to climb the high limestone cliffs and puzzle about Frank for a while, maybe even to ask his ghostly advice about some things that were bothering him.

There were unsavory stories in Texas as there were anywhere, about what could happen to a young woman unlucky enough to be stranded on a lonely road. If he didn't stop, the wrong man might. Hell, who was he kidding? Noble motives had little to do with it—not that he hadn't rescued a damsel in distress in his time. But Raven White wasn't known in these parts for passing up beautiful available women.

Most women smiled when his name was mentioned, but there were those who said "beware." Because no matter how much he enjoyed women, his affair with Astella had left a residual coldness in him which had prevented him from ever becoming seriously involved again.

Raven should have gunned his big black motorcycle and sped past the hitchhiker. After all, his friend, Pam, was waiting for him to come out to her ranch and make up their latest quarrel. But he still felt too mad at her to make up, and he had raced past Pam's ranch because even though he cared about her as a friend, he was tired of her demands. She wanted way more than he was willing to give.

Raven felt all mixed up about a lot of things—about Frank's death, about Pam, too. About himself for being so cold. His aloneness had become a loneliness that was getting harder and harder to stand.

He'd been thinking about California, about his father and Astella and his sister there, whom he hadn't seen in years, whom he hadn't wanted to see. He'd borne the rejection of his family with a dark bitterness until Frank's sudden death had changed his perspective. Many years had passed since Hunter Wyatt had kicked him out and disowned him, swearing he never wanted Raven to return. Raven was beginning to think maybe he should go back for a brief visit, just to make sure his father still felt that way— before it was too late. Frank's accident had taught him that death had a way of sneaking up. Frank's death had also severed his deepest ties to Texas and made him want to make amends with his family.

When Raven roared past the slim redhead, she wiggled her thumb at him again. He braked a hundred yards past the bridge and whipped the bike around, skidding wildly.

Pam wouldn't like this.

Who said Pam was running his show?

He thought of the way Pam had almost slapped him at Frank's funeral because she had wanted to create a scene in front of the largest possible audience so everybody would think there was more to their relationship than there was. Pam loved the fact that the whole town had been gossiping about them ever since Frank and he had taken her under their wings and hired her as their secretary almost as much Raven hated it.

What Pam didn't know was that he loathed his bad-boy reputation, which was due more to Old Lady Lescuer's malignant gossip than to anything he'd ever done. Of late, ever since Pam had decided that she was ready for the friendship between them to ignite into something more passionate, Raven had taken it into his mind that she was getting about as hard to take as Judith Lescuer.

Another look at the frightened girl in white was enough to make him forget Pam and Judith and speed back across the bridge. He hit the brakes when he reached the opposite side so hard he slid to a showy stop that slung wet river gravel violently. A chunk of rock and mud bounced off the redhead's ankle.

As she cried out and knelt to rub the injury, it began to sprinkle a little harder. With the heel of his boot, he jammed his kickstand down and swung his powerful body off the bike.

He was aware of the girl's involuntary clutch of fear as he stood up. In his black helmet and boots, he was very tall. Very muscular. Very tough. He probably seemed very much the evil character Judith Lescuer had painted him to be.

"You okay?" he asked, lifting his visor as he strode down the cliff toward the river.

There was no wrecked car in the ditch. No skid marks into the river. No bruises or gashes on the girl either.

She nodded shakily. "I-I'm fine."

The cool air was sweetly scented with cedar and the last of the season's bluebonnets.

His hard green gaze swept her. She went still, like a startled wild thing frozen in panic. Her distraught brown eyes seemed to blaze in her pale face. Were those raindrops or tears that beaded her thickly fringed lashes? Was she furious or sad? Or both? There were dark shadows beneath her eyes. He realized suddenly that she was violently upset—probably at whoever had dumped her out on the side of the road like so much garbage.

Aside from her fear of him and her anger, some deeper bruised quality about her drew him, gentled him. She was one of the walking wounded, but as she took a deep breath he sensed her fierce determination to conquer whatever explosive emotion was eating at her.

He knew that feeling; he was in the grip of it himself. Feelings like that drove one to do mad, desperate things. He felt that Frank's death was pushing him near some fatal crisis. Without Frank, his terrible loneliness now seemed unbearable. Raven, who prided himself on his fierce independence, felt new inexplicable needs. The same need that made him want to go home to his family drew him to this girl.

"You mind telling me what you're doing here all by yourself on the side of the road?" he demanded harshly.

She bit her lip, stiffening. "A . . . a friend drove off and left me."

"Some friend. A man?"

"You wouldn't believe me if I told you."

"Try me."

"Look—it really isn't important."

"Some jerk leaves you and—"

"Look—I said... It's really none of your business. Anyway, it was sort of my fault."

It irritated him that she defended the villain. "Then maybe I'd better just get back on my bike—" He turned to go.

"No, please— Wait! I appreciate your stopping." She eyed his motorcyle dubiously. "I do need a ride...at least back to Dripping Falls or to San Marcos."

"You were probably hoping some old lady in a fancy car would stop."

"Oh, no! Heaven forbid—"

But there was no denying the wild emotion that had flared again in her eyes.

"You haven't murdered one, have you?" he asked with a faint twist of his beautiful mouth.

The smile in his voice brought a tight curving to her pretty lips, too. "Of course not!"

His gaze was drawn to her eyes. He held up his hands. "I'm clean, too. It's a no—to murdering old ladies— however much a certain one or two has tempted me, or to any other crime."

She smiled. "But yes to grief and loneliness and despair."

How did she know that?

He was dressed all in black; she in white. Suddenly he realized how ferocious he must appear in his black leather jacket and gloves, in his helmet that concealed most of his face.

He unbuckled the helmet and ripped it off. Bareheaded, his curly black hair was unruly, and a damp swirl of it fell across his eyes. "As you can see I'm as harmless as any old lady," he murmured. "I'm no wolf—I'm a lamb."

One good look at his darkly carved face and she visibly relaxed. He grinned—because he was used to having that effect on the opposite sex.

"You're no lamb," she whispered, "but I don't think you're as big and bad a wolf as you might sometimes want people to think you are."

He frowned. "And what would you know about me?"

"Why... nothing," she said—but too innocently.

He didn't think his reputation had spread much beyond the city limits of Landerley and the domain of Judith Lescuer's wagging tongue. He had no memory of ever having seen this girl in Landerley before, and she certainly didn't speak with the local twangy accent. So it never occurred to him that she might have close connections there that he knew nothing about. That thought wouldn't come till he was caged in the numbing, solitary blackness of a cell made of steel bars and reinforced concrete.

At that moment, he was too charmed by the passionate intensity of her pale, frozen face, too dazzled by some fragile quality in her tight smile. Too mesmerized by the almost tangible animal attraction he felt for her.

"I'm glad you stopped," she said with startling intensity.

"Careful. It's dangerous to be too nice to a stranger, especially a man."

"Surely not to a lamb such as yourself."

Was she teasing him? "I have a confession. Most people would say I'm more of a wolf in sheep's clothing." That was putting it mildly.

"It's highly unlikely that you could ever be more dangerous than my own family or the men who've pretended to love me," she said quietly.

"Amen," he murmured on a bitter laugh, thinking of his own mother and then of Astella and his father and of Pam, as well.

The girl giggled rather nervously, catching herself abruptly. She was prettier when she laughed.

She looked past him, her brown eyes widening with alarm when she heard a car rounding the curve.

Raven turned too, just in time to see the yellow Chevy whiz past. Just in time to start at the sight of the burly man with a chopped, longish haircut, who sat hunched fiercely over the wheel. An old, unpleasant fragment of memory stirred. Noah... The driver looked like Pam's dangerous ex-boyfriend, Noah.

A rush of anxiety went through Raven. Then the beauty beside him sighed in relief when she saw Noah, and Raven couldn't help wondering who *she* had been expecting, who she'd been so afraid of and why.

The girl was wearing white silk—*wet* white silk that clung to her shapely breasts, narrow waist, and slender thighs. Maybe the long-sleeved blouse and slacks had been proper and prim looking before the lightly falling mist had soaked them thoroughly and plastered them against her shivering body.

Raven decided to worry about Noah later.

Raven peeled off his leather jacket, but she only backed away from him when he offered it to her, as if she were afraid of touching anything that was his.

He moved toward her, the black jacket in his out-stretched hand. "You're getting wet, right?"

With chattering teeth, she kept shrinking away from him.

"And you are cold? So—put it on," he ordered brusquely, losing his patience, and taking her arm gently.

"Then you'll get wet," she whispered.

"Honey, I won't melt."

She stood still as he helped her. His black leather jacket swallowed her. When she couldn't work the zipper, he helped her with that, too, at least till the thing stuck halfway up and his hand brushed her breast. Then he began fumbling, and, afraid that she'd guess why, he jerked his fingers away.

With wide shining eyes, she looked up at him. "Your hands are shaking. You are getting cold."

His blood pulsing hotly, he kept his resolute gaze on a cedar bush fifty yards behind her. "I'll be fine," he muttered as he leaned down and picked up the small, muddy duffel bag at her feet and slung it onto his bike.

At that she cried, "Hey, what are you doing?"

"You wanted a ride, didn't you?" He secured the duffel. "So—where to? And don't tell me just to Dripping Falls."

"To Austin. I have a plane to catch this afternoon."

"You picked a helluva time to have a fight with your boyfriend." Raven handed her his spare helmet and climbed onto his motorcycle. After she buckled it, she just stood there, as if she were contemplating the enormity of what she was doing.

"So—get on. I won't bite. I'm the lamb, not the wolf, remember?"

"That's not what I was afraid of."

When his eyes met hers, her frightened smile and the huskiness he'd heard in her low-pitched voice sent a savage dart of male excitement through him.

"Ever ridden one of these before?" he asked as she warily climbed on behind him.

"My mother always told me not to," came her warm breathy voice against his ear.

"And you were a good girl who did everything Mama said?"

"Oh, no—I'm not sure I've ever followed a single piece of advice she gave me," she admitted guiltily.

His kind of girl. "Hang on to me—tight."

She leaned into him and wrapped her arms around him, before reluctantly pressing her warm body into his. "Like this?"

He was aware of her legs spread as widely apart as his were. "Tighter," he commanded and was startled by the hot rush that went through him when she obediently scooted her parted thighs forward until her pelvis snugly molded his backside, until her legs strained against his. Desire for her raced through his veins and lit his nerve endings.

His fingers clenched around the bike's wet handlebars as he waited while her hands groped across muscle and bone and then the flat of his stomach and knotted at the center of his hard belly.

"This better?" she asked in that same uncertain undertone.

His throat felt so dry he could barely talk. "Much," he muttered, but the raw-edged syllable escaped through tight lips.

Not wanting to dwell on how much better, he gunned the bike so hard it bucked as it jumped onto the road. She screamed, clinging tighter. Which felt good. Too good. At least it felt good till the clouds darkened a few miles down the road and the storm winds rushed violently around them before the dark sky erupted. Then rain and wind pelted him from the front, while her soft warmth seeped into him from behind.

Not that it rained long. But they were both thoroughly drenched and shivering. By the time they pulled into a gas station on the edge of Austin, the sun had come out, and the afternoon was sparkling. When Raven was done at the pump, she came running out of the bathroom almost in tears because of the way the wind and rain had torn her hair loose and tangled it. Her wet clothes were wrinkled and smudged.

"I'm a mess. I can't fly anywhere looking like this," she whispered.

He glanced at her. She still had that half-scared look. But she was right. She did seem gypsy wild. Not so prim and proper. But cute. Damned cute. Not that he said so with words. But his eyes got hotter. "So where to?"

She scanned both sides of the freeway frantically and then pointed. "There's a motel over there."

He felt like he'd been punched in the gut.

"I have to shower and change," she said quickly.

"Of course," he said very casually.

But he didn't feel casual as he checked into the room while she stayed outside and watched his bike. And she was as tense as he was by the time he unlocked her door and lugged her duffel bag inside. He glanced at the two neatly made beds.

He wondered if she was imagining him naked in her bed amid tangled sheets—as he was imagining her?

Maybe so. Or maybe she just read his mind. Because she hurried him outside and shut the door in his face without a word.

He turned away, the thought of never seeing her again making him feel even darker and lonelier than he had at Frank's funeral, so he didn't notice when she opened her drapes and watched his broad-shouldered form move dejectedly toward his bike where he fiddled with his helmet an unconscionably long time.

He only noticed her when she came flying toward him with bobby pins in one hand and her hairbrush in the other. Looking up at the sound of her running footsteps, Raven was filled with overpowering elation. When he smiled, her answering smile was as bright as his. Then she came hesitantly forward.

She had unbuttoned a couple of buttons beneath her collar as if she'd been about to remove her damp blouse. The lower neckline emphasized the beautiful grace of her long neck.

She'd taken her hair down, and the red mass of damp silk streamed about her shoulders and her lovely neck. Wet white silk clung to her high rounded breasts. The vision of her in his bed came into sharper focus.

He wanted her. More than he had ever wanted any woman.

"I didn't even say thank-you," she whispered. "I didn't buy you gas.... Could I pay you for helping me out?"

"You don't owe me anything," he muttered, swallowing hard as she came even nearer. "I needed the ride, the distraction. You took my mind off my problems."

"You did the same for me," she said. "Thank you."

He forced his gaze from her body, and for a long moment he studied her pert nose with its dusting of freckles, the white skin and the almond blush at her high cheekbones. There was something very appealing about her. It wouldn't be hard for a man to grow fond of that face.

Odd thought, since she was a stranger; odder still to have such powerful feelings for someone he hardly knew, since he hadn't considered a permanent attachment to any of the women he'd dated for years.

"Well, goodbye then," he said in a thick voice, unable to resist the impulse to brush a strand of silken red hair from her eyes, liking its softness when it curled around his finger. "No more fighting with that boyfriend of yours in the car."

"Don't worry. I don't plan to see...*him*...any too soon."

"No more hitchhiking, either?" he continued in that same soft tone.

She nodded obediently like a child listening to a lecture.

"And good luck."

He pulled his hand away.

Her lovely face tightened; her mouth trembled. "I could do with some." Her voice was sad, lost. So were her lovely brown eyes.

Before her lashes fell, he imagined they were beaded with tears. The thought of leaving her suddenly depressed him.

He wanted nothing more than to take her in his arms and kiss her till she lost that look of sadness. He wanted to bury his face in that glorious hair, bury his flesh in her sweet, young body.

The fantasy was ridiculous. It wasn't as if he were hard up, where women were concerned. And it wasn't like he had a choice. This woman was a stranger. She lived a long way away. He had never gone in for long distance romances. He had to have a woman near at hand.

So they parted, both thinking that the pleasant encounter was the end of it.

If only he'd been so smart.

Or so lucky...

Three

Through the fog of pain and narcotics Raven White was barely aware of the sirens, of the ambulance doors being opened and slammed, of rushing feet all around him as he was wheeled hurriedly down long, brightly lighted hallways.

Only when the sensation of movement stopped abruptly did he pry open his swollen eyes and blink painfully beneath a harsh white light.

For a second he thought that the steady beam came from the guard tower. That he'd been crazy enough to try to go over the wall. That they'd shot him down.

Then a woman laughed softly and someone said, "Get serious, nurse. This is an emergency."

Where was he?

At first Raven thought he was back in San Francisco. It was the day of his father's wedding to Astella. Raven had gotten roaring drunk at the reception and abducted Astella in her wedding gown and veil. He'd forced her out on his father's boat and driven so recklessly, he'd wrecked it. Fortunately Astella was wearing a life preserver and had been thrown clear. When Raven had regained consciousness in the hospital, Hunter had said, "Too bad." To his lackeys, he'd issued orders in a rage. "When he's well enough to walk out of here—throw him out. Pay him off. I never want to see him again."

Raven had stumbled out of the hospital the next day. He'd changed his name. He'd tried to forget he'd ever been Hunter Wyatt's son.

The dream faded and Raven focused on the boots in blue, hovering near, working with more tension and feverish energy than usual. He remembered the long years in Landerley, Texas, the two years that seemed even longer in prison.

He couldn't make out the boots' faces because instead of their uniforms, they wore masks and ugly blue cotton caps. They had shiny knives instead of guns. Other weapons were massed on stainless steel trays.

One of the boots, the woman, stroked his brow gently. It was odd, a boot being a woman. Odd, the sensation of her kindly, soothing fingertips.

His mother had never touched him. Never hugged him. Maybe that was why he had such a weakness for a woman's caresses.

The human touch was something he'd done without in prison. The back of her hand lingered against his brow, coolly professional yet soft, its gentleness immensely comforting. Her compassionate dark eyes held a sympathy for him that no eyes had held in prison. More than anything else, the presence of this sweet woman made the aching loss of his freedom hurt all the more.

"Snake?" Raven gasped raggedly, hopelessly.

"I'm sorry. Your friend died a few minutes ago."

They'd say he was a murderer for sure now.

"Self-defense," Raven struggled to explain, so the others wouldn't seize him and throw him into the hole.

"Everything is all right, Mr. White. You're safe. But we've got to operate. You've lost a lot of blood, but you're going to be fine. Now if you would just count backward—starting from one hundred."

Then she placed a plastic mask over his face, and he was sliding away from the lights and her concerned eyes, away from her gentle touch and down that long black tunnel into his own inner hell, and he found the sweet hitchhiker waiting there.

How lucky Raven would have been if the pleasant goodbye at the motel had been the last he'd ever seen of the redhead.

If only he'd had the sense to head back to Landerley, back to work or even back to Pam. But he'd felt restless, and since he was in Austin he decided to stay. And part of the reason was he couldn't stop thinking about the hitchhiker.

His wet clothes felt heavy and sticky, so he drove to a nearby shopping center and bought a new pair of jeans and a shirt. Which, no doubt, he needed, since he wasn't much on shopping for clothes unless his old ones were so threadbare Pam started nagging.

Afterward he was so hungry he stopped at a hamburger joint not far from the motel where he'd left the hitchhiker. He got off his bike and carried his new clothes inside.

When he came out of the men's room in pressed jeans and a crisp blue shirt and was heading toward the counter to order, his dark gaze was drawn to a solitary figure sitting by the window. There was something about the girl's long neck, something about the severe little knot perched at the top of her head that made him look twice.

It was her—his sweet hitchhiker.

Blood pounded in his head like a jungle drum signaling danger. Which was ridiculous. Never in his entire life had Raven Wyatt been afraid of a woman.

He should have run.

Instead he stopped abruptly—in midstride—and looked at her for a long, silent time, his hands balling and stretching. Funny, her choosing the same hamburger joint he had.

The sun was setting and its fiery light came from behind her. She had the saddest, most vulnerable expression on her face as she studied two squabbling children near the door. Raven wondered what she found so fascinating and so disturbing about the feisty, little redheaded boy who was slugging it out with his sister over who would be ruler of the gum-ball machine.

Suddenly the boy shoved his sister too hard, and she and the gum-ball machine crashed to the floor. Only when their mother rushed toward them, did the redhead finally see him.

When Raven waved, she started guiltily. He imagined she would have preferred that their goodbyes at the motel be final, but he could hardly ignore her. He walked toward her table, determined to say hello and go.

But when he reached her table, she smiled. As he stared into her brilliant, welcoming eyes, he felt a thrilling jolt of awareness. All trace of sorrow had left her face; she was obviously glad to see him. Every bit as glad as he was to see her.

"Do you mind if I sit down?" he said, running his hand through the inky dampness of his hair, mussing the thick swirls he had just combed.

With shy eagerness, she removed her purse from the place next to hers, so he could sit there. "You look nice." She stroked the crisp fabric of his blue sleeve when he sat down and then drew her hand away, but not before his skin felt tingly from her pleasant warmth. Not before he realized she was trembling, too.

"Nice fabric," she said offhandedly.

"I went shopping. This is a helluva coincidence—our seeing each other again," he began.

There was an awkward silence. She looked down at the table and sighed. Then she dared to brush the top of his hand uncertainly, little guessing how her light, shaking fingertips unnerved him.

"Not really," she whispered.

Curious, he captured her slender wrist and intertwined his long fingers with hers. "What do you mean?"

"I was in a cab," she went on slowly, "on my way to Town Lake. I saw your motorcycle out front."

So, their goodbyes had frustrated her too.

"I told the cab driver to let me out. I don't know why, really. I just felt—"

She looked at him and then away.

And he knew. He felt her wildness, her loneliness. Because it was the same as his own. He pressed her fingers.

"It was an impulse," she said, trying to pull her hand from his. "I never do crazy things like this. I mean I never even go up to the attractive men I know at parties and start conversations. But I feel so funny today...strange, not myself, out of control. Like I want to rebel against who I am and everything I've been. Like I can't stand myself and want to be someone different."

"I know the feeling."

"God—my whole life is such a mess."

So was his. Ever since he'd lost Astella and his father had kicked him out, he felt abandoned. Until now.

Again her brown eyes were huge and vulnerable—naked.

And hot. So hot.

They scorched him with their heat.

"I feel so lonely," she said.

His large hand wrapped around hers tightly. He liked the way that small warm palm fitted his. "Don't apologize. You haven't committed a crime. I'm glad you're here. I was thinking of you, too."

"Really?" She blushed, disbelieving him.

"Really. I was wishing I had the nerve to go back to the motel and talk you into dinner."

"You—not have the nerve?" More blood rushed to her face. She bit her bottom lip and looked away. "Don't."

"What?" he demanded.

"Give me a break," she said. "I mean I can't imagine you lacking nerve when it comes to women."

He frowned. "Okay. So, I don't—usually."

"Is that another line?"

He started to bristle, and then caught himself. Was he being glib? Maybe she had him figured. Maybe he'd gotten so used to saying what would get him what he wanted, he no longer knew when he was being sincere.

Slow down, Raven.

Raven's hard, dark glance flicked over her, noting the bagginess of her jeans and the looseness of her overlarge green cotton blouse, which was buttoned all the way to her chin. Her damp hair was brushed free of tangles and screwed into that ugly, little knot at the top of her head again. She had taken great pains to make herself look as unsexy as possible.

But she had followed him. She wanted him. Even if she felt ashamed of her impulses.

"What happened to that plane you were supposed to catch?" he asked smoothly, determined to set her at ease.

"I put it off till tomorrow 'cause I was scared to fly," she said warily, avoiding his eyes. "You're probably not scared of anything."

He wasn't scared of the kinds of things she was talking about—physical things, like heights and planes and other men. But he remembered the scared, lonely feelings he'd had as a kid—the way his father had made him feel so worthless. He was scared of invisible things, like the emptiness inside him that made it almost impossible for him to reach out for love or return it. Suddenly he realized he was scared now—scared of the strange, inexplicable closeness he felt for her. "I like a woman who has me all figured out," he muttered. "That way I don't have to waste valuable time explaining myself."

"Well—me, I'm scared of a lot of stuff."

"Like what?" he murmured.

"I'm not a good flyer." She laughed shakily. "That's an understatement. I mean if I'm in the wrong mood I go berserk. I get claustrophobic. I'm scared of heights, too. If I look out the plane's window and see how small the houses and roads are, I start thinking—*I can't get out.* I'm five miles up here. Humans have no business flying. I start thinking about gravity and about what would happen if we lost a wing or an engine. I start looking at big people and wondering how much they weigh and how much freight we have on board. If I'm by the wing, I start watching the engines and imagining I see flames. I could go on, but if I do, I won't be able to get on that plane for a week."

He laughed. "This from a girl who hitched a ride with a stranger in black leather."

"Oh, that was easy compared to flying."

"Is that a compliment or an insult?"

"It's whatever you want it to be."

"I prefer compliments," he murmured.

"I . . . I suppose it is." She stopped herself. "The point is a lot of bad things have happened to me lately. My nerves are so shot today, I decided I needed to relax tonight."

"I'm glad you chose me to relax with."

Panicked color flamed in her cheeks.

"So—relax," he said quietly. "I'm just as new at this as you are. There's nothing to be afraid of."

Raven was about to ask her name when the redheaded little boy dashed back to the gum-ball machine. The hitchhiker's brown eyes darkened with the pain of some loss as they followed him. She paled, withdrawing her hand from Raven's.

"I came in here because I felt so alone," she murmured in a forlorn tone. "And I knew I'd just feel lonelier if I flew home to my empty house tonight." She was watching the boy. "But it's no use—running, trying to forget, 'cause you can't run away from yourself." She touched Raven's sleeve almost guiltily. "Look, I'm lousy company. Especially tonight. I'm sorry I bothered you."

She got up. To go. To leave him—again.

Then the kid stuck a nickel in the slot, and when his gum ball refused to come out, he began to bat the gum machine impatiently. She watched the child, paralyzed, looking more stricken than before.

Sensing there was no way he could compete with the kid, Raven grabbed her hand again. "Let's get the hell out of here."

She tried to argue as he led her outside. "Look, the last thing you need is me hanging on to you tonight."

He remembered Frank's funeral and all the dark misery and uncertainty waiting for him back in Landerley.

"Honey, you're very wrong," he said in a voice filled with warmth and compassion.

She was the only thing he did need.

"I don't even know your name," he said almost in afterthought when they reached his motorcycle.

She looked startled, almost dropping the helmet he handed her. "There's no need for names when all we could ever possibly share is tonight."

"Are you married?" he demanded, going cold.

She didn't answer.

"Don't lie to me," he growled.

"No." But there was a sad wistfulness in her voice. "Not anymore. And I haven't slept with anybody since I was."

"Then why the big secret?"

"I can't explain. I just want to be with you. Without strings. Without complications."

"Hey—that's supposed to be my line. And I'm afraid I don't like it much. I want you to explain."

"I was afraid of that," she whispered, leaning closer, setting his helmet firmly on his bike. "I didn't think a guy like you would care."

"A guy like me? What the hell is that supposed to mean?"

"When I was growing up, I . . . I lived in a house with a perfect older sister. I was the bad kid, the rebel, the kid who got attention the wrong way. I always got blamed for everything that went wrong. Even for my parent's bad marriage. And in the end, I really believed I was responsible. But secretly I dreamed of the perfect life I would have when I grew up. I began to work very hard to achieve this secret ambition. So hard that I spent my whole life weighing every action, making all the right choices, eating all the right foods, doing all the right exercises, selecting only the right people to become involved with—insisting on proper introductions. I got away from my parents. I had the perfect career, the perfect husband.... But do you know what happened? One fine day my perfect, beautiful life at the top of the world just blew up in my face, and hard as I try I can't seem to find any of the meaningful pieces. I feel dead to the bottom of my soul. So dead I'd do almost anything—just to feel alive again for a few precious minutes." She paused. "You make me feel alive. Is that so wrong?"

He'd felt dead since his father's wedding day.

"What does that have to do with not telling me your name?"

"Everything."

"Damn it, tell me—"

She lifted her sad, bitter eyes to his and did not speak, instinctively choosing the only path that could silence him. One of her hands went to the knot at the top of her head and she withdrew a single pin. Molten waves of fire spilled to her shoulders. She looked younger. Freer. Wilder.

"I liked it when you said goodbye and touched my hair," she said softly. "You have gentle hands."

When she closed her eyes and moistened her lips with her tongue, he knew she was going to kiss him. Just as he knew he should demand the answers he wanted before she did, but when she shook out her gleaming hair and her lush, wet mouth claimed his, he lost all power to reason.

At the first taste of her warm lips, a shock went through his whole body. Then her mouth parted invitingly, and somehow his tongue gained entrance and was exploring the delicious, welcoming cavern of her mouth. One of his hands tunneled through her perfumed hair to her scalp, while the other jerked her closer and aligned her slim hips against his.

She had a marvelous mouth. A marvelous body. And wonderful hair. She fitted him perfectly.

Prim and proper had been an illusion. He felt the wildness in her beating just beneath the surface, and it stirred the old wildness in him, too.

An electricity came from her and burned him, too. One long seeking kiss and he knew he had to have all of her.

Not that he could take her in a public parking lot.

Their tongues mated. Her lips sucked his—one last time. "You're delicious," she murmured, pulling away reluctantly, as if she knew she'd given him just enough to whet his appetite. "So—do you want tonight...?" She clung to him tightly as though she felt dizzy.

"Who are you?"

"You must choose—you can have me or my name."

"Blackmail is a dangerous game."

"I don't mind playing dangerous games. The question is—do you dare play, too?"

"Tell me who—"

"What are you so scared of? Just choose, my sweet, nice wolf...or is it my harmless lamb?" she whispered teasingly, nibbling his mouth delicately one last time, setting him aflame with kisses and her tongue arousing the wolf in him and subduing the lamb.

He licked his dry lips and found the moist, hot tantalizing taste of her lingering there.

But he was more lamb than he knew, because with her lips and her kisses, he let her sell him a one-way ticket to the slaughterhouse.

Four

The night with the sweet hitchhiker that preceded the nightmare of prison was one of the most wonderful in Raven's life. It was as if some perverse demon had granted him a glimpse of heaven before casting him into hell.

In the beautiful hitchhiker's company, all sorts of simple things seemed to take on a special glamor. They went to the grocery store where they pushed their cart down the wide stacked aisles, laughing together like eager children as they picked out steaks and salad makings, chips and soda. Every time their eyes met and their hands brushed, his excitement built. He could almost forget his dark grief when she was near.

Then he drove her to Zilker Park and barbecued steaks over a grill. The night was clear and studded with stars, and a waxing moon shone through the lush leaves of the towering pecan trees. Because of the darkness he burned the steaks, but they happily ate them anyway.

After dinner they walked beneath the tall, rustling trees along the gravel path by the sparkling river, holding hands like lovers. They could hear the sounds of the city; they could smell the damp, sweet, woodsy scent of the trees and the river. He talked to her, spilled out the loneliness in his soul, while she, who did not say much, merely listened.

Without naming names or places, he told her about his childhood, how his wealthy father and famous mother had had no time and no love to give him, how he'd grown up feeling lonely and worthless, how these feelings had intensified after his mother had died and his father rejected him, how when he'd finally found love in the arms of a beautiful older woman, his father had seduced her and married her.

Raven told her of the agony he'd felt on his father's wedding day as he'd watched the golden Astella marry Hunter Wyatt and his millions, how Raven had gotten drunk at the reception and asked the bride to dance, intending to pour out his love. But she'd refused him even a dance, and in a rage, he'd seized her and run. Crazy with jealousy and determined to prove his love, he'd taken her out on his father's boat only to wreck it and nearly drown. His father had thrown him out after that, and he'd wound up on the road.

One of the people he'd hitched a ride with had been Frank Clark. Frank had brought him to his ranch outside of Landerley and given him a job. Raven had worked very hard and prospered, even though there were a few people who hadn't approved of his methods. He told her that Frank's son, Doug, was the closest thing in the world he had to a friend.

Raven felt an easiness in her company, as if he'd known her for years. She got quiet when he spoke of Frank's death and how depressed he was because if he'd ever loved anybody it had been Frank. She grew even quieter when he spoke of the Lescuers, especially Judith, and her irrational hatred of him and Frank; quieter when he told her how ironic it was that the two men from these enemy camps had driven into each other head-on. But somehow Raven found a depth of understanding in her silence, feeling that she knew first hand how terrible a sudden death could be.

He got off the grim subject, apologizing for it, but she took him in her arms and held him for a long time. And he found a deeper comfort than he'd found with Pam or Doug, both of whom he had known for years, both of whom shared his grief; a deeper comfort than he'd ever known in his life. After that he took her riding on his bike through the cool, sparkling darkness, out into the countryside over roads that curved through sweetly smelling cedar-covered hills.

From the highest hill, they looked down on the glittering miles of city spread beneath them like millions of diamonds. The tallest buildings were outlined with lights, and the Capitol, awash in floodlights, seemed the grandest of all.

Beneath that black sea of spinning stars, he kissed her again, bumping noses at first and laughing with her at his initial clumsiness, before his mouth found hers and claimed it properly. This awkwardness at lovemaking was new to him, and yet somehow it had to do with the special tenderness he felt for her. He kissed her then, passionately and deeply, neither of them shyly uncertain any longer, both of them finding fierce glory and pleasure in this innocent step toward what had been inevitable from the first moment he'd seen her standing in the mist on the side of the road.

When they returned to town she told him that she wasn't ready for their evening to end, that what she wanted more than anything was to go dancing.

He was no good at dancing. But he knew she was suddenly afraid of going back to the motel with him, and since he was in the mood to oblige her anything, he took her to a crowded club that he'd heard of but never been to before.

It was the kind of place where strangers meet and dance. She asked the band to play her favorite song, "Wildness."

Raven sat by himself at a dark table in a corner and drank a beer while he watched her dance alone at first beneath the colored lights and then with a variety of partners. Maybe he should have felt green with jealousy because he was no dancer and the other men were. But he was sure of himself in other areas, and he knew he could handle the men if they got too familiar.

She had told him that because her domineering mother had made her take a million dance lessons as a child, she loved to dance. She was very good, and the longer he watched her body sway beneath the lights to the music, the thirstier he got.

Finally she refused every man who asked her. Instead she came to his table and took his hand and begged him to dance.

"The last girlfriend I went dancing with said I was a lousy dancer," he murmured.

"Different woman—different tango. Maybe we'll be good together."

"More likely I'll stomp on your feet."

"Maybe I'm in the mood for a dangerous adventure."

He took her in his arms. When it was put like that, so was he.

He pulled her into the shadows away from the others. The first step he took landed on her toe.

"Sorry," he whispered. "I told you I was no good at this. Do you want to sit down?"

"Maybe all you've needed was the right partner. Just relax," she ordered. "Feel the music."

And her hand undid a couple of buttons and slid inside his shirt against his hot skin. With a silken fingertip she thrummed the rhythm against his muscled chest, her hand stroking the carpet of dark hair that grew there.

At her touch, all of his anxiety slid away. Her body melted into his; together they melted into the music and became part of it. She began to move in a way she had not moved with the other men, closer against his body, her dance intended to arouse.

It did. She did.

His breathing grew ragged. He pulled her deeper into the darkness, liking this dancing thing as he never had before....

It was very late when they roared up to her motel on his motorcycle. On the dance floor, she had been graceful. At her door she fumbled in her purse for her key.

Suddenly growing impatient, he took the key from her and unlocked her door, holding it open so she could go inside. He stepped in after her.

The air-conditioner was blasting, and the tiny room was dark and cold. She flipped on the lights and paled at the sight of the two turned-down beds and her damp clothes and intimate apparel scattered about on the chairs and dresser to dry. He noted with a smile that she carried enough makeup for ten women.

"I-I usually pick up after myself," she murmured, her voice unsteady as she reached for a lacy bra and a filmy pair of panties and tossed them nervously into her duffel bag. "But... I was too upset." She began to smooth the bed and adjust the drapes. She turned up the thermostat. When she began neatly lining up the makeup bottles in front of the mirror, he seized her hand, brought it to his lips and blew a kiss through her fingers.

"You still are—upset," he said quietly, releasing her. "I'll go now, if that's what you want."

She drew a quick breath. Her dark eyes burned him. "Scared, too?" she whispered, trying to tease in spite of her fear.

Eager. Wild. Those were better words to describe his attraction for her. But he was scared of this deeper thing he felt between them.

"I've never done this before. Never even wanted to," she admitted.

Why was he so glad of that, when he'd never see her again?

He caught her to him, his hands stroking her tumbled hair soothingly. "And you don't have to tonight."

"Kiss me," she whispered. "Just kiss me. I won't be afraid if you kiss me."

Her mouth was red and wet.

She closed her eyes expectantly.

Swiftly he shut the door and turned off the light. And without the slightest difficulty, found her again in the darkness.

"I know you've had a lot of women," she whispered.

How could she possibly know that?

He frowned, glad she'd never heard of his exploits with women. Most of all he was glad she hadn't heard all the lies.

"So this won't mean all that much to you," she went on.

He bent his head and nuzzled the perfumed silk of her hair. "Shut up," he commanded, wrapping his arms around her. "You mean more to me than you know."

"You really don't have to say things you don't mean. I'm not a child."

His grip tightened. "Damn it. Don't be stupid."

For a long time he held her, saying nothing, his hands caressing her. Slowly the tension drained out of her, and she began to follow a more compelling instinct.

"I wish I could believe you," she said, her voice filled with intense, sweet longing.

Her first tentative kiss fell upon his shoulder as softly as the flutter of a butterfly's wings. The warmth from those gentle lips and her breath seeping through the crisp cotton to his skin was unbearably erotic. Then her innocent mouth moved lightly across his chest, leaving a tingling path in its wake. She paused to explore the throbbing hollow of his throat with the tip of her tongue. His pulses went mad as her fingertips slid upward along his jawline and raked into the thick swirls of his black hair.

Even when she drew his flushed face down to hers and his body grew hard and his breath heavy, he remained still, not kissing her, fighting his fierce desire.

"What's wrong?" she whispered, looking up at him, her face softly flushed now, her hair loose and wild.

"Nothing. I just don't want you to be scared. Not of me."

Her hand slid down to the waistband of his jeans and unfastened the first button. Her fingers moved inside and down across warm muscle and hard bone to claim intimate possession of him. "I'm not scared any more."

"You are beautiful," he rasped. Then she touched him more boldly and turned every part of him to fire. "Too beautiful."

Her fingers circled him and stroked him, and his control shattered. A fierce groan of arousal erupted from his throat. Crushing her to him, he kissed her lips, softly at first, deepening the pressure only when her hands came back around his neck, only when he felt her entire body begin to tremble. Only then did his tongue plunge deeply inside her.

Their mouths clung. For a timeless moment, it seemed that she was utterly and completely his.

His hands spanned her slender waist, lifting her easily with strong arms, holding her high above his head, reveling in her dainty and yet voluptuous beauty as he slowly lowered her, his mouth tracing the length of her abdomen and then the lush curves of her breasts where he paused, burying his face between both soft globes for a long moment before lowering her the rest of the way.

Their bodies fused, every male nerve in his body screamed to possess her. Never before had he been so strongly aroused . . . so dangerously involved emotionally.

It was too soon.

All other women had been to satisfy an appetite. But she was different. Even though she was a stranger, he felt a powerful oneness with her that went beyond mere physical desire.

Profoundly excited, he pushed her against the wall, his body pressing into hers, kissing her throat and lips until he could barely breathe. Then he stepped back. Unbuttoning her blouse and jeans, he slid them to the floor. Hurriedly he tore his wallet from his pocket and flipped it onto the bed. Next he ripped off his clothes.

Then they were in bed. He kissed her lips, her face, her nose, her ears, until she was sighing breathlessly and begging for more. Only in that last moment did he remember he had to protect her. While she lay beneath him, he fumbled to find his wallet in the tangled sheets, struggled with the wrapper as she kissed his throat and then his lips again.

When at last he was gloved, he came into her swiftly, pausing when her hands dug into his shoulders so he could savor the tight velvet warmth of her soft body joined to his. A savage rush of sweet fire pulsed through him. Holding her, and being inside her, gave him more pleasure than he had ever known.

Still he waited until she pressed her hands into his back, until she arched her body and urged him deeper. Only then did he thrust inside her again and again, and she followed him, her body moving in perfect harmony with his. Together they peaked and died in that final primitive explosion that was the most glorious and sweetly satisfying of his life.

Afterward when she wept, he cradled her close, feeling powerful and strong.

"What's wrong?" he whispered.

She rolled on top of him, her tears falling one by one onto his cheeks. "I-I'm not sure." Her hair spilled over his sweaty shoulders, sticking to his warm, wet skin. With her hands she gently framed his hot face as if he were very dear. Her tearful gaze lovingly traced each feature—his eyelashes, his nose, his mouth.

"I-I can't believe this," she said.

There was an intensity about her that frightened him.

"Why are you looking at me like that?" he demanded.

"I'm memorizing you." She smiled wanly. Then more great sobs wrenched her body. He pulled her close, stroking her.

"The last thing I wanted to do was make you unhappy," he whispered.

"You don't understand. It was wonderful. *You* were wonderful.... I was married for years, and nothing like this ever happened to me before. I'm afraid I made my husband very unhappy—especially in bed.''

"Hey, it couldn't have been all your fault."

"Yes, we both agreed it was." She was silent for a while, staring at him. "There's more. A long time ago I lost someone, and I've never been able to cry. Till now. You gave me so much—ecstasy and this gift, this wondrous relief from grief. I'll treasure tonight and the memory of you forever. You cannot know how terrible the pain was, how much I needed to let some of it go."

He stared into her sparkling eyes, and their loving warmth made him feel wonderful, cherished. He wrapped her more tightly against himself, and she continued to cling and weep while he gently held her.

"Who are you?" he whispered. There was something about her mood that bothered him. "I have to know. I want to be more than a memory. I can't let you walk out of my life tomorrow."

"Don't talk." She pressed his lips with her fingertip. "Just hold me," she said through more tears. "Hold me tightly—forever."

Gradually her sobs lessened, but she stayed where she was, nestled against his warm, muscular chest, clinging, until finally she slept peacefully, her head pillowed by his shoulder.

No woman had ever felt so right. No woman had ever made him feel so strong or so needed; so worthy and complete. No woman had ever given him such pleasure in sex, nor such spiritual bliss afterward. Nor such profound communion with her soul.

She stirred but didn't waken when he kissed away each and every tear before kissing her gently on the lips—one last time.

His final confident thought before he fell asleep beside her was that at last he had found the one woman he had been searching for all his life. At last he had found someone he could love. He knew he could never let her go.

In the morning he would find out who she was. Then he would ask her to marry him.

But in the morning she was gone.

Instead, two policemen with drawn guns and hard voices were banging on his motel door, threatening to kick it down.

As Raven yanked on his jeans and stumbled to the door, he didn't yet know that he had gone to bed with an angel in paradise only to awaken in hell.

Then he threw open the door.

The two officers stood like giants blocking the sunlight.

The first dreadful sentence that registered on his startled brain was, *Raven White, you have the right to remain silent.*

Raven stepped back stunned, unable to believe this was really happening to him. Even when they shoved him against a wall and held him there spread-eagled, their rough hands searching him, even when they jerked his hands behind his back and cuffed his wrists, some part of his mind still refused to accept it. Even when they hurled him into the backseat of their patrol car, caging him in like an animal, his feverish brain screamed in denial.

"Do you mind telling me what the hell this is about?" he asked.

The younger cop's blue eyes were as cold and hard as ice. So was his voice. "As if you don't know."

The other cop said, "You're wanted for the murder of your girlfriend—Pam Hatch."

Five

Innocence Lescuer clutched her stomach when the jet hit still another bump. Then she pulled the shade so she wouldn't have to see the rain violently streaking against the window.

She had known she shouldn't come.

Two years ago Innocence had sunk to her white silk-clad knees, rather melodramatically, too, in the mist at Scud's Crossing, and sworn on the exact spot where her father had died that she'd never return to Texas. She had been so furious at her impossible mother that she'd been sure she had finally learned her lesson, that no matter how hard she tried she could never get along with her mother. Apparently her mother felt the same, because Innocence hadn't seen or heard from her since. Not that Innocence hadn't checked her mailbox and her answering machine every night after she had finished caring for her neurosurgery patients and come home.

So why was Innocence a terrified passenger in an airplane circling Austin? Why was she risking not only her life but her fragile, newfound happiness as well?

Was she really just doing what she'd always done—desperately seeking the approval of her crazy, domineering mother?

And if her impossible relationship with her mother wasn't reason enough to stay away, the danger of a chance encounter with Raven White, Landerley's number-one real-estate shark and womanizer, was.

Raven White had been Innocence's one, fateful lapse into the precarious world of sexual liberation.

Not that *he* would remember her. Not that *he* would care even if he did. No doubt, he'd had countless women since her.

Since her mother was the self-appointed authority on the lurid love life of Raven White, Innocence had known who Raven was and what he was as soon as she caught her first glimpse of his huge muscled body racing toward her on that motorcycle. Furious at her mother, Innocence had held her thumb out—feeling some instant bonding with this man her mother hated more than any other.

He had certainly lived up to her mother's billing.

Not that Innocence, who had been frigid for years before he'd cured her, had any regrets.

On the contrary. She would be grateful to him for the rest of her life.

But he was one man she never wanted to see again.

The jet bounced in the turbulence, and Innocence caught her breath, clutching her sleeping baby daughter, Ashley, more tightly. Innocence stared in wonder across the aisle at the nerveless Marcie, Ashley's young nanny, who was dozing as unworriedly as Ashley. How could

Marcie sleep through this storm, when any minute they
might all die?

The plane hit another rough pocket and plunged. Ashley woke up with a thrilled giggle, stood up on her mother's lap and jumped up and down. Like her father, she had
a streak of the daredevil. And the thought of that father
was enough to make Innocence quiver with real fear.

Dear God. She did hate flying, especially in the rain, and
she was glad she had lowered the shade so she wouldn't
know for sure she couldn't see the ground. Their plane had
been circling for an hour.

The plane dived again. If her sister, Linda, hadn't said
their mother could die, Innocence would never have flown.
Except for her father's memory, she felt little closeness for
her family. As a child she'd tried to win her critical mother's love. Failing and feeling guilty, she'd longed for
nothing more than to escape her. Which Innocence had
done by becoming a neurosurgeon, marrying Matthew and
moving to San Francisco.

Even after her divorce Innocence had rarely returned to
Texas, the last obligatory time having been her father's
funeral. Again she had tried to make peace, but her jealous mother had been annoyed that she'd come for the funeral and not to see her, and had spent the week making
her feel guilty.

Thus, when she and her mother had set out for Austin
that fateful afternoon, Innocence had been eager to leave.
When they'd reached Scud's Crossing, Innocence had
pulled over for a final look at the dangerous curve that
dipped into fog and nothingness, where her father had died
the week before.

She'd been saying a silent prayer for him when Judith
had burst jealously, ''Wipe that sentimental look off your
face. Your father was drunk when he hit Frank. Not that

Clark didn't deserve to die. May they both burn forever in hell."

"Mother, how can you—"

"And don't always act so horrified by everything I say. You're just as thoughtless as your father. You ignored me like he did, the same as you ignored Matthew and Timmy. You don't know how to be part of a family."

Innocence cringed inwardly. "I've tried—Mother. You'll never know how hard."

Besides melodrama, Judith had a flare for judgmental religion, and her mood was vengeful. "If your father hadn't been drunk, Frank would be alive. Last year if you'd been home where you belonged instead of playing God at that hospital, Timmy would be, too. You killed your own son, the same as your father killed Frank. Timmy's death was the Lord's vengeance for your monumental ambition and neglect."

Desolation filled Innocence's heart as she remembered her bright, lively, beautiful, redheaded Timmy. Innocence couldn't think of a single defense, because she blamed herself too. As Matthew had.

Innocence set the parking brake, and grabbing her mother's keys stepped out into the gently falling rain. "Maybe I felt I had to be a doctor and work hard to prove I was of some value to the world. Maybe I never learned to be a mother because you were never a mother to me. Because you never loved me the way you loved Linda."

"Because you were always your father's child, and Linda was mine."

Innocence felt a prick of guilty remorse because she had loved her father more. It began to rain harder. She was getting wet.

"Close the door and get back into the car. You're ruining my leather upholstery."

"So you can crush me with more guilt. No thank you!"

Innocence slammed the door defiantly and ran down toward the mist floating up from the river, thinking to calm herself for a minute or two. Then she heard the Cadillac's engine and realized that her mother must have had a spare set of keys.

The car door was opened and slammed. Innocence's duffel bag hit the shoulder with a thud.

Innocence made it back up the hill in time to see the back of her mother's silver head and her jaunty wave as she drove off.

At the sight of her duffel bag in the mud suddenly all Innocence's rage drained away, and she felt curiously weak and defeated, which was normal after a few days of her mother. Innocence sat wearily down on her duffel bag, not caring that she muddied her white silk slacks or that the silent rain soaked her hair and clothes.

Her only son was dead. So was her father. She had never been able to get along with her mother or her sister. They both blamed her for everything, and maybe they were right. Still, there seemed nothing she could do to change that now.

Never had Innocence felt so alone.

But she couldn't cry. Since Timmy's death, the explosive grief and pain had been locked up inside her. Even though she'd fought to save Timmy, his other doctors had told her Timmy had never had a chance. But when he died, she still blamed herself and quit working for several months. Sheer willpower had made her return to work.

Now her father's death seemed to compound the grief she felt for her son.

God, help me, she prayed.

An eerie breath of air stirred the vapors sifting upward from beneath the low water bridge. The distant purr of an approaching motorcycle broke the vast stillness.

The purr became a roar. She stood up just as Raven White leapt out of the rain and mist, as if in answer to her supplication. Even with his helmet covering his face, even though she'd never seen him before, Innocence recognized him instantly. He was the one person her mother criticized even more than she criticized Innocence. And almost before she thought, Innocence had sprung to her feet and stuck out her thumb.

She was almost relieved when he drove past. When he stopped and turned around, her pulse raced out of control. Her fear of him warred with the thrill of him when he roared back, skidding up to her. He jumped off his bike like some great, graceful jungle predator.

He was huge. Enormous. An immense male creature, every sleek part of him laced with rippling, lean muscle.

She was sure he couldn't possibly know who she was. Her parents had moved to Landerley after she was grown. Her visits to her parents' ranch had been too brief and infrequent, and she usually went into Dripping Falls or San Marcos instead of Landerley to buy staples because her mother had fallen out with all the Landerley storekeepers. Judith had quarreled so bitterly with the local mortician that Sam had had to be buried in San Marcos, thirty miles away.

Judith had described the flamboyantly handsome realtor in maliciously vivid detail.

"His shoulders are so massive and broad he looks like a giant. He has a swarthy, hawklike face, and he prefers black to any other color, so that he looks more like a satanic specter than a man. He has a black truck and a huge black motorcycle. You know what those are extensions of—not that I'm saying *they say* he needs an extension—''

Raven White had sold her parents their ranch. Her mother, who had liked him at first, had later decided that the price she had paid was too high and had demanded a great deal of her money back.

When he and his partner, Frank Clark, had refused her, Judith had begun digging up as much dirt on Raven as possible and then retold every story with new twists that put him in the worst possible light. He had tried to stop her, and when he couldn't a feud had sprung up between the Clarks and Lescuers, who were actually neighbors as their large ranches came together at one corner.

Most of the citizens of Landerley had sided with the Clarks, and Judith had been disliked more than ever.

When Raven got off his motorcycle, with that aura of smoldering male sensuality around him that rainy afternoon, Innocence had thought him every bit as wickedly forbidden and tantalizing as his legend.

''You mind telling me what you're doing here?'' he had demanded in a wonderful, virile baritone that had sent shivers through her.

She had stammered some nonanswer, knowing better than to admit she was any kin to Judith or Sam Lescuer.

Raven removed his black helmet and she had got that first compelling view of his turbulent green eyes, his midnight dark curls. One glance at his darkly chiseled face and she had decided to find out for herself if he was as dangerously thrilling as her mother said he was.

His sudden white smile had aroused in her the kind of molten excitement she'd read about in novels, and she was plunged from grief and guilt into flustered agitation. As a teenager she'd never had a crush on a football player, and she had no experience with a man who was so ruggedly male, no experience with a man reputed to be the best of lovers. She knew only that he made all other men, even Matthew, seem dull in comparison.

Never before had she felt so wild with curiosity to get to know someone, such a delicious fear that made her tremble. And as Raven began to talk and tease her kindly, when he wrapped her in his jacket, the soft black leather still warm from his body, and invited her onto his bike, where she had clung to him with the wind and rain whipping around her on that most glorious ride, when he gallantly left her at that motel and never made a single fiendish move to seduce her, she forgot her mother's stories and fell under his spell.

Had he been the Lord's vengeance her mother believed she deserved?

Or the answer to her prayers?

The answer to both questions was an unequivocal yes.

Alone in that bleak motel room after he'd gone, she had thought of Timmy and Matthew and her failed relationship with her own family, and guilt and loneliness had closed over her.

She'd showered and dressed and then collapsed across her bed, craving nothing more than to know again the delicious warmth she'd experienced when she'd ridden behind Raven on his motorcycle. Then she remembered all the intelligent reasons for sending him away, the chief being that he would hate her when he found out who she was.

She had called a cab and headed into town, doubting there was any place she could go where she would feel better. By chance she had spotted Raven's motorcycle at the hamburger joint. Her dark spirits had lifted, and she'd lost all pride and rushed inside.

And when Raven had first seen her, the intense welcome in his eyes had stirred her soul.

He had known how to take things from there, known how to sweep her on a dizzying tide of desire to a fulfillment she had never even dreamed of. And afterward, she had found the release she had craved so long from the dark emotional bondage of her guilty grief.

The next morning when she'd awakened in his arms, she'd wanted nothing more than to stay there. But they had agreed on one night. She hadn't wanted to risk seeing the disgust in his eyes when she told him who she was. So, she had loosened his arms. When she'd kissed him goodbye, he had smiled in his sleep, and mumbled two words very drowsily.

"Sweet Hitchhiker."

Gathering her things, she had dressed hurriedly and run, little realizing how irrevocably changed she was. Little knowing when she reached California that she'd left some precious, vital part of herself behind. No matter how hard she tried, she hadn't been able to forget him. She would lie awake in her bed, remembering the hot sweetness of his hard lips and gentle hands.

Maybe it was her hopeless yearning for Raven that had made her friendlier to her ex-husband, Matthew, with whom she had gradually formed a new attachment.

But when she found out she was pregnant, she kept this precious fact a secret even from Matthew, who came from a stuffy, well-connected family—one of his cousins was even married to the governor of Texas.

Before Innocence started to show, she went away to have the baby secretly. After the birth, and with the help of a therapist, Innocence finally forgave herself for Timmy. She no longer blamed herself entirely for her failed marriage, and she forgave Matthew, too. She invented a story that one of her patients who had no relatives had made her the temporary guardian of her only baby daughter, saying that when the patient had died, Innocence had adopted the baby.

It seemed a supreme irony to Innocence that a man such as Raven White was responsible for her release from guilt and for her profound new happiness.

Innocence would be grateful to him forever.

But he must never, never know.

Although Innocence had disciplined herself and only rarely thought of Raven now, her attraction to him had been the most powerful emotion in her life.

But Raven White was a womanizer; the night they had shared would have meant little to him. She could not risk the stable future she planned for her child by having anything to do with him.

She'd felt safe about her new life until her sister had called and begged her to come home. Safe, until she'd started dreaming of Raven again. Safe, until she realized that she had never stopped longing for him.

What if she did run into him? Would he even remember her? What would he do if he discovered who she was? If he found out about Ashley?

None of her mother's stories held a clue as to his feelings about children.

She would have to be very, very careful.

Ashley was dozing quietly again, and Innocence stroked her black curls, frowning as she remembered her sister's desperate call, the first from her family in nearly two years.

"Mother's had a heart attack. She might be dying, and we're having an awful time with her doctors."

"Does Mother want me?"

"Well, I'm sure if she were feeling better—"

"The truth, Linda."

"You simply must come anyway."

Why must she? Her mother had driven off and left her. She'd never bothered to call.

But deep down Innocence had known she had no choice, because no matter how she might tell herself she didn't care about her mother, she did. If she didn't go, she'd feel guilty about it forever.

The plane hit another bump and jolted Ashley. She stood up sleepily, again bouncing up and down in Innocence's lap. "Mama..." She rubbed her eyes and then reached for the window shade and tried to pull it up.

"Darling," Innocence said gently, stopping her. "We're not going to treat each other badly when you grow up. I'm not going to make you feel guilty about everything you want to do. Not ever."

Ashley's green eyes sparkled as if she agreed. Then quick as a flash she reached up and playfully tweaked her mother's nose. "Mama." Then Ashley lowered her head and hid her face in her tiny hands, so Innocence couldn't tweak her nose back.

Around the crown of that small lowered head, the baby's hair grew in thick black swirls.

Ashley had *his* hair. *His* eyes. *His* powerful beauty and incredible, magnetic appeal. And *like* him, she knew it.

Ashley peeped through her fingers and said "Mama," again. Mama had been Ashley's first word, and Innocence's heart filled with love every time she heard it.

At fifteen months, Ashley was the most guilelessly charming, the most exquisitely lovely miniature human on earth. She was terribly precocious. At least her mother thought so.

And so did Matthew, who had slipped a diamond ring on Innocence's finger and asked her to marry him again right before Innocence and Ashley had boarded the plane.

The pilot told them to prepare to land.

Innocence held on to her daughter, and said a silent prayer.

"Please, God, don't let anything destroy my second chance at happiness."

Then the jet struck the tarmac so violently, even Ashley screamed. A few minutes later they stepped out into the storm. The dark skies reminded Innocence of Scud's Crossing and the day she and Raven had ridden his motorcycle in the rain.

Maybe because she was in Austin again and holding his daughter in her arms, the memories of the man who'd taught her to love came into sharper focus. And the poignant loss she suddenly felt was more powerful than ever.

She still wanted him.

And because she did, she felt an awful, impending sense of doom.

Six

The gray-haired woman behind the bank of computers at the reception desk kept typing when Innocence walked up.

"Excuse me—please. Would you mind telling me what room Mrs. Judith Lescuer is in?"

The hospital volunteer looked up warily. "Who wants to know?"

The hand Innocence had placed on the counter balled tightly. "Innocence Lescuer. I'm her daughter."

"Didn't know she had another daughter."

That hit a nerve.

Innocence took off her reading glasses and glared at the woman.

"Not many people do. But I'm a neurosurgeon from San Francisco, and I've come to check on her."

"Well, you've got your hands full, Doctor. That crazy bunch has had the hospital in an uproar ever since they got here. Which was two days ago, although it seems like a week."

"My mother's room number—please!"

"Room 332. Not that she'll be there long. She's already changed rooms six times. First she said she was too near the elevators. Then she didn't like the nurses on 2A. The fourth room was too small. The fifth's television set was fuzzy. Now it's her roommate. And that's not all. She's refused to be transferred to Austin because she's against the heart bypass her doctors recommend."

"Do you have any good news about my mother?"

The receptionist looked blank for a minute. Then her seamed face brightened. "She's threatening to walk out AMA."

AMA stood for against medical advice.

"Thanks for the room number."

"Try to talk her into Austin."

Innocence cringed when she heard her mother's carping tone behind the door. Her mother certainly didn't sound sick.

"I don't know why these idiots stuck me with a jealous, old sourpuss like you, Lula. You always have had it in for me—even before I figured out your no-good friend, White, had swindled me—on your behalf."

White... Raven... White. Guilt and panic clawed inside Innocence.

Of all the bad luck. Her mother's roommate had to be Lula Clark, Frank Clark's wife.

Raven himself might be in there or come at any time.

Dear God. How could she go in?

"And who in Landerley doesn't hate you for all the mean lies you spread, you insecure, pretentious, sanctimonious, old windbag?" Lula demanded in a low voice that slowed to emphasize each unflattering adjective. "Doug, are you going to get me moved or not?"

Doug Clark—Frank's son.

"Just as soon as they can get a private room ready, Mother," came Doug's low-key baritone.

"If it takes more than fifteen minutes, I'll be dead."

"No such luck. With my delicate heart and the way you keep attacking me, it'll be me!" Judith blasted.

"Me—attacking you?"

"Yes, Lula! Which is entirely unjustified. All I have ever done is speak the truth. Such as—you aren't sick. You faked that fall to get in here, so you'd have some company and get waited on. I never knew a more demanding tyrant in all my life."

"Take a look in your mirror, then. And since you're so fond of the truth—it was your malicious ways that drove Sam to drink. Which means you killed my Frank."

"How dare you blame me for Sam! Thou shalt not judge. You haven't the slightest idea how that man abused me for forty-one years!"

"If only he had—"

"Enough! Both of you!" This thunder came from the deep-voiced Doug.

Doug was known to be as lazy and easygoing as Raven was intense. It sounded like the two old ladies had him pretty frazzled.

Innocence swallowed glumly. She couldn't go in. Not when her mother had the Clarks in such a stir. Not when Raven might come at any minute.

But as Innocence turned to leave, a young nurse pushed the door open. Then Linda saw her, and it was too late to run. Judith turned pale.

The atmosphere was so charged with hostility that Innocence felt as if she'd stepped into a powder keg. All that was needed was a spark.

Both Clarks regarded her coldly. Especially Doug.

Apparently Innocence was that spark.

Linda embraced Innocence coolly. "I told you to call first."

Judith attacked Linda. "What's she doing here?"

"I came to help, Mother," Innocence replied.

Doug Clark was staring at Innocence with a fixed, obsessive expression.

"Go away!" Judith hissed to her daughter. "You should know I don't want you here. You've never done anything but make me miserable."

Hurt in spite of herself, Innocence backed guiltily toward the door and began to fidget with the knot on top of her head. And as she pried a bobby pin open with her teeth, she happened to meet Doug's steady blue gaze. He hadn't once taken his eyes off her since she'd walked through the door.

Nor did he now.

Disconcerted, her lashes fell.

His didn't.

He was tall and golden. Landerley folk said he was easygoing. Judith said he was lazy. There was nothing relaxed about him today. Not that his fascination seemed sexual. No, it was more that of a bounty hunter, who having memorized a most-wanted poster, had finally found his prey.

Innocence went back to her mother's bed and yanked the privacy curtain, cutting off his view.

Had Raven known who she was, too? Had he seduced her as a joke and then bragged to his partner's son about his conquest?

Judith's petulant voice broke into this disturbing train of thought. "I want you to go back to San Francisco—immediately."

Innocence wanted nothing more. "I came because Linda said you were very sick. Mother, this time I hoped that we—"

"You were probably hoping I'd die. Which I may do if you don't leave."

Innocence sighed.

"Mother, I thought Innocence could talk to your doctors," Linda soothed. And then to Innocence, she whispered, "Give me a minute to talk to her."

Innocence nodded, grateful for the reprieve, until she became aware of Doug racing to catch up to her as she walked hurriedly toward the nurse's station.

He grabbed her arm. "Not so fast."

"What do you want?" she demanded.

His arm fell away. "You tell me."

"You keep staring at me like I'm a ghost."

"Maybe you are."

"What's that supposed to mean?"

"Why didn't I know Judith Lescuer had another daughter?"

"We . . . we don't get on. She doesn't exactly go around bragging about me." *Why had she admitted that hurtful truth?* "I don't get to Texas very often."

"So, when did you last get to Texas?"

"Two years ago for my father's funeral."

He went white. "The same weekend my father died," he said in a quiet deadly tone.

He was scaring her with his vengeful voice and hard blue eyes. "Look, I guess you're Frank's son, Doug—"

"You guess—" he snarled softly. "Don't pretend you don't know. It's no secret your mother runs us down to everyone she meets."

It didn't seem loyal to admit such an unflattering truth about her mother. "Look, I'm sorry about your father," Innocence said gently, "but the accident was terrible for us, too."

"Don't pretend you think that's all this has to do with—"

"What are you talking about?"

"You set up my best friend!"

He was talking about Raven White!

Doug seized her arm and pushed her toward the wall, but before he could do more Linda came up to them. "What are you two doing?"

Innocence swallowed. "Mr. Clark, do you mind?" She stared at the bruising hand he had on her arm. "You're hurting me."

Flushing, Doug released her. "We'll finish this later."

Innocence sagged against the wall and rubbed her bruised arm.

"Are you going to tell me what that was all about?" Linda asked quietly.

Innocence's mouth felt dry. There was no way she could ever admit what had happened between her and Raven White. "He didn't say."

"Well—" Linda frowned. "Good news. Mother said that forgiveness is divine, and that since you came all this way the least she can do is be generous and let you apologize.

"*She'll let me*— Linda, what did she tell you about our quarrel?"

"That you said she was a terrible mother. Innocence, how could you attack her with Daddy just dead? . . . You knew she was grieving. You broke her heart. She came home in tears, and she's been so upset ever since, she hasn't once allowed your name to be mentioned."

As always Judith had made herself into the victim. As always Linda fell for it. As always Innocence was the guilty party.

"Now remember, Innocence, she looks stronger than she is. Promise me, just this once, that you'll be kind to her and apologize sweetly."

Innocence approached her mother's bed and placed a tense hand upon her mother's. Judith's thin smile held triumph.

"How do you feel?" Innocence whispered, guiltily aware of Doug Clark on the other side of the curtain and aware, as well, of Linda's expectations.

Judith's thin mouth tightened. "Linda said you were going to apologize. I'm waiting...."

Control. But some fragile thread inside Innocence snapped.

"Maybe I feel you should be the one to—"

Linda frowned worriedly. "Innocence, remember, Mother's sick. You agreed—"

Innocence bit her lip and tried again. "In the heat of anger I, er, well, I may have made a few critical comments...about the kind of mother—" Another fragile thread of control shredded.

It was no use. She couldn't lie. "I said what I said because you made me feel terrible about Timmy, the way you've always made me feel terrible about everything."

"What I said was the truth. You were cruel and unfair to attack me for not being a good mother."

"You drove off and left me! In the middle of nowhere! I had to hitchhike to Austin. I was lucky the guy who picked me up wasn't a maniac."

Suddenly the curtain was ripped back.

Doug flew at her in a rush. *"So it was you."*

"Don't listen to him!" Judith grabbed Innocence's hand and frantically pulled her closer. "I'm sorry, dear, but don't, please, don't tell these people a thing. They've never liked us. They've been absolutely awful to me ever since Sam died. They've made up the most dreadful lies about me. I can't even go into Landerley anymore."

Her mother's guilty expression filled Innocence with a strange dread. "Mother, what is going on here?"

"As if you don't know," Doug thundered.

"Mother?" Innocence pleaded.

Her mother pulled her sheet to her nose and cowered behind it.

Innocence whirled on Doug. "Mr. Clark, I don't have the slightest idea what you're talking about."

"Are you, or are you not—the sweet hitchhiker?"

Dear God.

Sweet hitchhiker.

The phrase brought back that last delicious moment when she'd lingered in Raven's arms, when she'd kissed him and he'd rasped those very words against her lips.

They had haunted her.

What had Raven told Doug?

Innocence managed a thin veneer of calm. "What did you call me?"

"What everybody hereabouts called the woman Raven claimed to have spent an entire night with—during the hours Pam was murdered and he stood accused of her murder—the sweet hitchhiker!"

"Dear God— You can't mean—"

Vaguely she was aware of her mother squirming deeper beneath her sheets.

"The nickname that made all the headlines, the nickname you, as well as all the other Lescuers, must have known about and gloated about. Raven claimed he picked up a girl at Scud's Crossing and drove her to Austin. She was his alibi. Only the next morning when he was accused of murder, she had disappeared. Nobody remembered them together. And nobody but me and Mother believed him, since he didn't know her name or where she was from or any other relevant detail about her."

Because she had refused to tell him.

Doug was still talking. "Everybody knew Raven hadn't been dating anybody special and that Pam had been chasing him, and they all knew she'd gotten furious at him at Dad's funeral because he'd refused to see her. It was me who told him to go out and make up with Pam. It was because of me everybody knew he was heading out to her ranch that day."

"I swear I didn't know any of this."

Doug's eyes glittered. "I was subpoenaed as a hostile witness, to testify he was on his way to Pam's. Because of you, I was forced to betray my best friend."

A cold chill swept Innocence. "What happened to him? Where is he?"

"As if you don't know! He's in prison. He got sixty years."

Innocence felt sick. *Prison...* Thick, salty tears blinded her.

Doug's contemptuous drawl cut through Innocence's pain. "It was you, wasn't it?"

Innocence's stomach tightened, and for a moment she was afraid she really was going to be sick.

She stumbled from her mother's bed to the window and undid her hair, coiling it tighter and tighter, tugging painfully at her scalp. When she repinned it, a silken strand fell messily against her wet cheek. Rattled, her hands shaking, she kept fiddling with her hair.

Raven had gone to prison for murder.

Because she hadn't known.

Because she hadn't come.

Because her mother, who hated him, hadn't told her.

No wonder her mother had never called her.

Innocence could scarcely breathe. She had betrayed everyone—her own family...Raven. As Innocence stared unseeingly out the window, she felt she was flying to pieces inside.

Linda whispered, "Innocence, why don't you just tell him it wasn't you?"

Because that's a lie.

"Yes, do that." Her mother's voice was muffled by the sheets now covering her face.

Innocence whirled on them both. "How can you say that, Mother? When we both know—"

She saw Linda's mortified face. Doug's triumphant one.

Dear God, what had she done? She was throwing her whole life away. Ashley's, too.

But Innocence couldn't stop herself.

Linda began to tremble then. "Never in my wildest imagination when I kept reading about the sweet hitchhiker did I imagine you could be her. I thought White was lying, or that it was some tramp. You've always been so prudish. So careful about your friends. Your men had to pass dozens of ridiculous tests. They all had advanced degrees and millions of dollars. They were sweet to animals. They were concerned about the environment. They were always so predictably, so politically correct. So *dull.*"

"But you knew differently, didn't you, Mother?"

Innocence went and knelt beside her mother's bed. "Mother, why didn't you call me? Why didn't you tell me he was in trouble? I know you hate him...and you disapproved of what you guessed I'd done, but..."

Her mother had buried herself so deeply under her sheets and pillows that, except for a tuft of gray hair, no part of her was visible.

"Why, Mother?"

Choking and gasping, Judith grabbed her heart. "You always were such a bad little girl. But this is the worst, the very worst thing that you have ever done. I will never forgive you."

"I don't know if I can forgive you either, Mother."

Judith's hand jerked wildly from beneath the sheet and sent one of her monitors crashing to the floor.

Then she cried out she was dying.

Seven

The sky was an ugly, leaden gray, the same color as Watchtowers Three and Four, where guards with rifles stood ready.

The prison's tall brick-and-cement walls topped with razor wire loomed forbiddingly above Innocence as she trudged behind Tom Holt, Raven's hard-bitten, cynical lawyer, and Ed Jeffries, the thin, rather wimpy-looking prosecuting district attorney, through a high chain-link gate.

As she entered the grim fortress, a feeling of utter hopelessness seeped into her.

Because of her, Raven White was locked inside.

Because of him, she had Ashley and her newfound relationship with Matthew.

Innocence would have given anything to oblige her mother who really had suffered a second heart attack, by refusing to see Raven. But Innocence had no choice. She had to help him.

No matter what it cost her. Or her family.

She tried to ignore the guards, ignore her sensation of terrifying powerlessness and guilt as the keys jangled in the metal locks and the heavy steel doors banged shut and were bolted. But every new noise jolted her, even the sound of her own echoing footsteps. And as she was led deeper and deeper into that windowless, airless human warehouse, she grew claustrophobic.

Her mouth was dry; she could barely swallow. She couldn't let her courage falter. She had to remember that Raven White had been locked in here for a much longer stint.

A guard led them into a dank cell, now used as a visitors' room, and locked them behind the steel gate. There was a small table and four metal chairs. After the dark hall, the overhead light was too bright; it made the pale green walls gleam a sickening opalescent color. Because the glare made her eyes ache, she sank down in the nearest chair and buried her face in her hands.

After what seemed an eternity the guard returned. He stared hard at the lawyer and the district attorney.

"Sorry. White says he prefers solitary to the two of you." The guard's smirk seemed to indicate he agreed with the prisoner.

"Did you tell him we've got new evidence?" Holt demanded, taking charge.

"He says you didn't do nothing for him when he was framed, and you damn sure won't now that he's taken the rap for killing Snake."

Innocence shifted nervously. She hadn't wanted Raven to know she was here until he came to the cell.

She pulled a crumpled slip of paper from her purse and scribbled two words. Then she handed the note to the guard. "Give him this. He'll come."

Because more than anything, he would blame her and want revenge.

"What did you write?" Holt asked after the guard was gone again.

"Sweet Hitchhiker," she whispered in a dull, lost voice.

The light made the men's white faces seem harsh and forbidding. She felt the unspoken condemnation in their eyes. Turning away, she grabbed the bars and peered down the length of the hall. Her stomach felt tight, nauseous. She dreaded this interview. If only she could have gotten what she wanted some other way, but the district attorney had said there was no other way. He had wanted to come, to see Raven's first unrehearsed reaction to her. To make sure she was telling the truth.

Innocence watched the guard's shadow flicker eerily against the wall as he disappeared down that endless darkening tunnel.

Then the bleak walls of that cell seemed to close in on her. She felt as if she were suffocating. Her heart raced. What had it been like to live in such a cage for a year, when she, who still possessed the freedom to leave, felt buried alive? She pressed her hot forehead against the cool bars and closed her eyes.

She turned wearily back to the grim-faced men. "How could something like this happen? How could an innocent man be locked up in this place?"

"White's no innocent now." This dark pronouncement from Holt.

No wonder Raven had refused to see him.

"You're his lawyer, but you thought he was guilty," she said in disgust. "Didn't you?"

"Since you say so, maybe he didn't murder Hatch. But he killed a man here and stabbed two others. He's a killer now."

"No!" she cried. "He's here because of me."

"All the guys in here are users. White's like them. He's used a lot of people in destructive ways," Holt persisted. "His land only went for the highest prices. He had plenty of women. You included."

"I don't believe all those stories were true. Even if they were, they wouldn't make him a criminal."

"A lot of people don't like White, and they're none too happy you turned up."

"Look, I know that. I've gotten threatening phone calls from some guy who keeps warning me to stay away from Raven because this guy doesn't want him out."

"They don't understand how you couldn't have known about the murder till now—you being a Lescuer and having family here."

"I told you how it is with my family. This isn't the first time my mother and I have taken a two-year... leave of absence ... from one another. Besides that, she falls into the category of those people who don't like Raven White."

"After White was indicted, people wouldn't have anything to do with him. His land deals went sour. When you didn't come forward, he got meaner—meaner than any of us would have ever believed," the lawyer continued, while the prosecutor nodded grimly, silently concurring.

She couldn't blame Raven for not wanting to see them.

"Then he jumped bail because the trial was going against him, but someone tipped the authorities and bounty hunters brought him back in shackles and leg irons. People decided then that he was guilty. They remembered how he'd never said where he came from, and a rumor got started he'd probably been running from the law. After he started doing time, word filtered back that he was brawling in prison. After he was accused of killing another inmate, only a few people in Landerley believed his story."

Jeffries kept on nodding in silent agreement.

"What was...Raven's story?" Innocence asked.

"Said he didn't remember killing anybody. Said if he did, it was self-defense. But the two that got wounded said he came at them like a crazy man and tried to hack them to pieces with a sixteen-inch shank."

"I believe Raven," Innocence whispered.

"Not that it matters. Even with your new evidence, I don't think we'll spring Raven White till he's old and gray."

"How can you sit there and say that so smugly, like he doesn't matter? You put an innocent man behind bars. You have to get him out! Do you understand me! Or I'll never be able to live with myself."

"What I'm trying to tell you is that White's acquired a long record of violence since he got here. The first week he hit a guard. Every time he got out of lockup, he'd get mad and get into trouble again."

"What would you do if you were innocent and you got sixty years for murder?"

"I'm trying to prepare you for the man you're about to meet. Raven White hates everybody now—everybody here and almost the whole town of Landerley. But the person he hates the most is you."

A shuffle of slow footsteps and the jingle of chains came from the end of the hall. She clutched the bars tighter, straining to see, listening as the horrible metallic sounds grew louder.

The prisoner was dressed in white and shackled, his hands cuffed to his waist as three guards marched him toward her. His broad shoulders were slumped. His arms dangled hopelessly. His black head was lowered. She couldn't see his face, but his posture and slow gait were those of a broken man.

Then with a furtive glance so brief she wondered if she only imagined it, the prisoner's narrowed, hate-filled gaze consumed her before he looked down, his eyes growing cold and soulless again.

A chill went through her as Raven was pushed into the cell. When he stumbled over the threshold, a guard cursed him and shoved him down. Raven staggered, his legs buckling as he collapsed at Innocence's feet.

In an attempt to pull him to his feet, another guard jerked a chain, wrenching the prisoner's shackled arms.

"Don't, please— He's not an animal," Innocence said, kneeling beside Raven. "Dear God, what have they done to you?"

At the sound of her voice the black head sagged lower, the broad shoulders hunched even more. When she tried to touch him, he sprang away from the hand she offered and slowly pulled himself up by the bars.

Her sorrow-filled eyes widened. He was so dirty and ill kept that he smelled. His once healthily tanned skin was prison pale; his hard jaw was shadowed with dark stubble. His cheek was bruised and his bottom lip was swollen and cut. He seemed to have shrunk in stature by several inches. Nothing about this poor creature reminded her of the virile man who'd made such passionate love during that wild, dreamlike night that still haunted her.

At the same time he hardly seemed the dangerous criminal his lawyer had described. Prison had crushed him. He was a weakling, afraid now of his own shadow.

She had to help him. He was in here as much because she'd been too stubborn to call her family as because of anything her mother had done. He was Ashley's father.

"I'm sorry," she whispered, reaching out to touch his arm. "So sorry."

Raven saw her pity and screamed savagely, recoiling from her gentle hand as violently as a wild beast from a branding iron. When the guards wrestled him to the floor, his shackles clanged against the bars. As he swung wildly to evade the guards' blows, his chains struck her wrist so hard shards of pain exploded from her injured wrist all the way up her elbow. Even as she turned white and gasped, she felt sorrier for Raven than for herself.

"Don't hit him again," she pleaded. When one of the hulking guards raised his arm, she threw herself in front of Raven, shielding him with her slim body even as he shrank from her nearness.

"White hit you," the guard spat in a rage.

"It was my fault. I never should have touched him."

A terrible quiet fell. At the ready for more violence, the angry guards stood poised over their cowering prisoner and his fragile protectress.

Nobody moved. The lawyer and district attorney grimaced, their disgust for Raven evident.

Slowly the violent tensions eased and the guards withdrew. Innocence stood up warily and brushed her dress free of dust. Raven dragged himself to his feet, too. Then he hurled himself as far from her as he could manage and began to bang on the bars of the gate, howling to be let out and taken away from her.

Not once did Raven turn back as he was led away from her, but Innocence watched him until he disappeared into the darkness. And even after that she listened to the rattling sounds of his chains dying away.

In the car Jeffries said, "Surely, Miss Lescuer, even you can see, he's where he belongs now. He's far too violent and too unpredictable to be set free, where he'd be a danger to himself and to society. Worst of all—*he'd be a danger to you.*"

"Just say the word—and we'll drop this unpleasant business and leave him right where he is—*where he belongs,*" Holt said.

Raven held Innocence's note to the light and looked at it one last time before wadding it up and pitching it into his foot locker. He pulled out a freshly laundered white uniform. Then he took out shaving foam and the razor a guard had loaned him.

The three creeps who'd put him away, the girl and his lawyer and the district attorney, were coming again.

Since he'd banged on the bars and screamed for them to get him away from her, Raven had thought of nothing except her.

How he'd hated the pity in her eyes.

All night he'd lain awake on his bunk, studying the delicate swirls of her handwriting, touching the black ink and the paper in wonder, imagining her slim hand scribbling the words quickly, carelessly, indifferently.

Raven lathered his face. He didn't have a mirror, but he'd grown used to shaving without one.

She was still beautiful. He hurt just thinking about her. He hated that, too.

As he raised the razor to his jaw, he tried not to think about how fragile and vulnerable she'd looked as they'd led him down that long dark tunnel toward her. Dressed all in white, with the brilliant light gleaming from behind her like an aura, she had seemed an angel. And yet sad...and frightened . . . for him. Even with her flame red hair, she hadn't looked in the least like the witch he'd convinced himself she was.

That hair. It was glorious. She'd worn it up yesterday in that ugly, little knot he hated, but he remembered how that wildly curling, glorious mass of silk had looked when she'd taken it down right before she'd kissed him the first time, how it had spilled over his hands and the pillow when he'd bedded her later.

His loins stirred hotly. God, why did she have to be so beautiful? Why did she have to seem so sweet, so remorseful?

She'd filled out. Her body had a womanly maturity that it had lacked before, but she hadn't lost whatever quality it was that made him wild to have her, which was crazy since she'd destroyed his life. Since maybe she was even an accomplice to murder.

She had the sweet face of an angel, but the hair and body of a temptress. Maybe it was the combination of innocence and sweetness and wildness that drove him mad.

With deft strokes he sliced through the white foam. He had willed himself to forget her.

He swished the razor under the tap, and then started shaving his jaw.

Funny, how seeing her yesterday had been enough for him to know she was unforgettable.

He stripped her in his mind, torturing himself with the memories of ripe breasts carved of smooth, molten flesh. He knew her taste, her smell. He remembered her every little whimper; he remembered how she'd clung so tightly to him.

Never had any woman felt so right.

He had wanted her forever.

But she had run.

And because she had, he'd lived in hell.

He had believed her to be a betraying witch. Yet when the guards had started to beat him, she had protected him.

And in that moment, he had known that the beautiful witch he longed to punish still had a dangerous stranglehold around his heart.

He washed the razor and yelled for the guard, who came quickly and took it while Raven scrubbed his face clean with a towel. He stripped and dressed in new whites, and all the time he thought of her.

He couldn't let her dupe him a second time. He remembered Noah driving by the day he'd met her. How scared she'd been of the car until she'd seen Noah. *She was a liar, a consummate actress.*

But she had come back, and she was coming again. And he felt incredibly different because she had.

Twenty-four hours ago his future had seemed so bleak he'd wanted to die. In punishment for Snake's death, he'd been placed in solitary.

Bitterly depressed, Raven had fallen into a quiet and withdrawn state. He had lived from meal to meal—stale sandwiches tossed into his cell three times a day.

Until *now.*

Until *her.*

Now he knew he had always wanted to live. He wanted his freedom. He wanted his life back.

And he wanted revenge.

The girl was the key to all three.

He would use her as she had used him.

He would stomp out the pity in her eyes and replace it with fear.

Who was she? Why had she set him up and run? Was she an accomplice to murder?

If he ever got out, she would pay.

Again Innocence ignored the district attorney and lawyer and held on to the bars while she waited for Raven.

As a neurosurgeon she had seen dying patients make spectacular recoveries in the space of a day. But never had she seen quite such a miraculous improvement as Raven's.

The figure who stepped boldly out of the shadows toward her seemed taller, his tread surer, his uniform whiter.

The shackles were gone. He had showered and shaved. No longer was the black head bowed in cowardly defeat. No longer did he shrink from his guards.

At first she was thrilled—until she saw the cold loathing in his eyes.

When he strode into the cell he planted his feet widely apart, looming so huge the other men seemed to shrink beside him. His green eyes impaled her, as if he were master now and she his prisoner. He laughed when she shivered, sick with dread and fear of him. Then he shifted his hard gaze to his former lawyer and the district attorney.

"How touching," Raven murmured coldly. "My three favorite people—together again."

"Look here, White, we're here to help you," Holt began.

"Like you helped me before."

"Look here, White, Jeffries and I are busy men—"

"Right, nailing poor bastards like me— Now Jeffries, here, his racket is a little different from yours."

Jeffries seemed to shrink beneath Raven's withering gaze.

"Jeffries used me to make a name for himself. He came off looking like a tough prosecutor when he stuck me with sixty years on a case that was based on the strongest circumstantial evidence the judge had ever seen."

"White," Jeffries yelled, "I don't have to take—"

"Shut up! I'm not through." Raven's beautiful mouth curled jeeringly as he regarded Innocence. "And you—"

She trembled when his glittering gaze raked her. The knowledge in those cold eyes made her turn pink with shame. He had seen every naked inch of her.

His grin broadened. "No," he taunted icily. "I didn't forget you, sweet hitchhiker." He wondered angrily if she'd slept with Noah, too.

She flushed. "Don't call me that!"

"What's your real name, then?"

Her breath caught. Defensively she arched her head higher on her long slim neck. "Lescuer."

His hard face grew colder. "Judith's daughter?"

"Sam's, too," she added quietly.

"Why am I surprised?" Raven's laugh was forced, as if some terrible joke was on him, and the cold sound sent chill down her spine. "What's your first name—honey?"

"Innocence."

"Oh, that's rich.

"And what about Noah?"

"I-I don't know a— I swear I didn't know—"

"Shut up," he growled, thinking of Noah's brutish hands or her body. "Whatever made me imagine for one second that you were warm and loving, you ice-hearted little witch? You have the wrappings of a sweet, passionate woman, but you're a liar like your mother. You refused to let me know who you really were because you were setting me up—"

"Oh, please... That's not true."

His scathing look told her he would never believe her.

An ugly smile spread across Raven's cold face as he turned back to the men. "Lucky for you three that I'm a forgiving man."

He extended his hand toward Holt and shook his lawyer's hand. Next he pumped the district attorney's.

Then Raven pivoted and extended his hand to Innocence. Had it been offered in friendship, she would have taken it. Instead, the blood drained from her face. Defiantly she knotted her hands into fists and kept them at her sides, refusing to make the phony gesture of politeness he wanted.

But he seized her hand, his large fingers brutally closing around the white gauze at her wrist in such a crushing grip she cried out.

"I've lived in hell because of you—Innocence."

When she tried to pull away, his grip tightened. "Don't think you'll escape me so easily this time."

He drew her closer. So close, the heat of his towering, hard-muscled body made her feel faint. His eyes blazed coldly.

He hated her, and yet his fierce hatred was somehow unexpectedly, dizzily exciting. It made her feel alive, as Matthew's affection did not. It made her hope—for something terrible and utterly forbidden.

"I-I'm sorry for what happened to you," she said. "You'll never know how sorry."

"I don't believe you—Innocence Lescuer." He drawled her name with softly chilling menace, as if he despised her. "Do you think I give a damn how sorry you are? Do you want to know what it's like to be locked up in a cage, in a sewer filled with savages—to die a little every day, until there's nothing left of the man you were?" He shook her hard. Only when she cried out did he stop.

"It would be a claustrophobic hell I wouldn't wish on any man. Especially not an innocent man... Especially not you," she whispered.

"Then why did you put me here?" he demanded softly.

"I didn't know until just now. You don't know how much I hate myself, blame myself."

He jerked her closer, and again his powerful dislike produced that warm, forbidden tide of expectant feeling in her.

"You're a liar, honey. Even worse than your mother. Because you pretend—"

"No!" she cried. "I didn't have anything to do with what happened to you. You gave me a ride—"

"You gave me one, too, remember?"

She flushed. "You were kind...when I needed kindness. I left because my mother had told me stories about you that made me believe you were the type of man who would want me gone. I would have given anything to stay, but I had no claim on you."

His face grew colder. "Don't lie to me. Nothing you say will make me forget or forgive what you did. Nothing will ever make me believe that Judith Lescuer's daughter ever wanted more than the pleasure of making me suffer as much as possible."

"I want to help you."

"Get me out of here, then. Not that I'll let you get away with setting me up. Tell me this. Were you in on Pam's murder, too?"

"No!"

"That's a little hard to believe."

"A lot of things are. You were found guilty on circumstantial evidence. You were innocent. Don't repeat the injustice with me."

"You're breaking my heart." His gaze smoldered. "You do deserve the same justice I got, and I've had two long years to think about what I'd do to you if I got the chance."

In spite of his fury and the utter coldness in his face, his passion drew her. Her pulses had begun to beat in her throat. She turned away—terrified.

* * *

Later, when they were in the car driving away, Holt advised her again to leave Raven in prison.

She tried to think of Matthew and her new relationship with him.

Instead, she thought of Ashley and her sparkling green eyes: Ashley, who was so filled with enthusiasm about life; Ashley, who loved everyone.

Ashley, *his* child.

And Innocence wondered if Raven's cold eyes had ever held the same zest for life as his daughter's, before a hard fate had twisted him. Could his eyes ever light again with warmth and wonder and expectation and love?

Could she kill the frigid hate and soften him?

She had thought she was through blaming herself for everything that went wrong in the lives that touched hers. But because of her mother she had been part of this terrible injustice to Raven.

Holt had said Raven had killed a man and that there was nothing they could do now, that leaving him in prison was the smartest course.

But as they sped away she turned back and looked at the forbidding grim fortress and tried to imagine being shut up inside it for sixty years.

He would die.

She remembered the desperate hour when she'd been alone at Scud's Crossing, when she'd felt so lost after her father's death and her mother had accused her of destroying her own child.

Raven had come and been kind and gentle.

And passionate.

He had not abandoned her.

He had changed her life and taught her to believe again in the power of love.

She could not abandon him.

Eight

There was a slickness about the way Raven's truck took the curve, twisting up the hill, that demonstrated how well he remembered the road from Scud's Crossing to Landerley.

"Funny you wantin' to drive out to Scud's Crossing first thing after seeing your house," Doug said lazily from the passenger side of the truck as they left the Blanco River behind them.

"Not so funny, if you think about it," Raven drawled coldly, remembering how angry and depressed he'd felt at the sight of his dilapidated house, weed-infested grounds, broken windmill and sagging fences. Doug had let the Clarks' ranch go, as well as most other things he'd promised to look after.

Raven needed to buy an ax and a chain saw and some other tools. "I went to Scud's because I wanted to see the exact place where a redheaded witch who looked like an angel sold me a one-way ticket to hell.''

"You know, Raven. I've been thinking. I don't think Innocence had anything to do with Pam's murder."

Not by the flicker of an eyelash did Raven reveal how intensely he disagreed. He stared ahead, his expression unreadable, his dark emotion carefully leashed.

"I mean—I know she's a Lescuer, but I can't believe she's a real criminal. Now, I agree with you that the Lescuers are a jealous, gossipy, hard-to-take bunch. But I never heard of 'em going so far as to break laws."

Raven's cold face was unyielding. "Keeping silent while I was railroaded comes close enough for me. If Innocence had nothing to hide, why didn't she come forward when she knew I was in trouble?"

"Maybe it's like she says. Maybe she did fall out with her mother. That'd be easy enough to do."

Raven pulled the brim of his black Stetson lower, to shield his eyes from the sun. "Or maybe she liked the idea of me going to prison as much as her crazy mother did."

Doug tried again. "She doesn't seem much like Old Lady Lescuer. I did a little snooping. You know Innocence doesn't get on with her mother. The Lescuers are a divided bunch, because Judith's always falling out with people and expecting her family to fall out, too. If they don't, she turns on them. Innocence and Sam both tried to stay out of Judith's squabbles, and to Judith that meant they were against her. Apparently she's laid one hell of a guilt trip on Innocence."

Raven was frowning, as if at the glare on the road ahead. His eyes narrowed on the flying cedar-covered hills. "You seem to have become quite an authority on Innocence. You seen much of her?"

Doug flushed. "Some. I was pretty hard on her the day we met. After what she did for you, I felt I had to make up to her."

Raven couldn't account for the sudden dark quickening of resentment he felt toward Doug.

Raven grabbed his sunglasses from the visor and put them on. He wasn't used to so much light; he'd lived without it too long. "Define 'some,'" he said casually, and yet not casually at all.

"Oh, I took her to dinner a couple of times. She's right pleasant. Not that there's anything between us, if that's what's eating at you all of a sudden. All she wanted to talk about was you. She feels responsible for what happened to you."

Raven stiffened. "I couldn't care less if there was...something between you."

"Good. Then you won't care that she's reengaged to her ex-husband."

"So, the lady likes to repeat her mistakes." Cold anger flared in Raven's eyes.

"She fought very hard to get you out. She got that brilliant former federal prosecutor to take your case without pay when the sheriff, the district attorney, even your own lawyer were all set against you."

"Hey, I don't need you to tell me that—"

"Even so, if her ex-husband's cousin wasn't married to the governor, you'd still be behind bars."

"'Cause two murdering liars say I killed a piece of scum who tried to kill me."

"She and her well-connected ex got you out."

"It took her long enough."

"A month. Record time, any way you cut it. Maybe you should be grateful."

Raven felt numb inside. And worthless. Prison had taught him he was a number, no better than an animal that needed to be chained and locked up. It had made him feel alienated from the human race.

"Doug, don't tell me how to feel, how to think, how to act. I got too much of that in prison. They strip search you three times a day. They read your letters before you do. They take everything from you—your privacy, your possessions, your choices, your privileges. The only thing they can't take is what's in your head. They just twist it around till you don't know who you are anymore."

"Sorry. I was just trying to help."

"You have helped. And I appreciate all you've done. You've been my only friend. You've stood by me the whole time, even through the worst. Visiting me in prison, in the hospital, picking me up this morning, bringing me my truck, gettin' my bike fixed up, offering to let me work for you till I get back on my feet. I don't know how to say thanks."

"You would have done the same for me."

Raven stomped harder on the accelerator. He felt like driving forever. He wanted to run—the way he had before—when his old life in California had become unbearable.

And he could have, if he took a mind to—all the way back to California. He could do anything he wanted. Choices. He had so many of them now. That was the thing. The thought of such freedom filled him with a strange joy, and the joy was followed by new doubts and tensions. Choices were a hard thing. So was happiness. He had been unhappy so long, he couldn't deal with the joy his new freedom gave him. He didn't trust it. His mouth thinned as he thought of the past twenty-five months. He focused his mind on the woman he was determined to

blame for the hell he'd been through. And the cold anger
that was easier to handle came back.

Because of her, he was trapped in Landerley. He
couldn't leave till he figured out how she fitted in this
thing. Only then could he start over somewhere else. He'd
have to put California and his family on hold for a while.
Hell, he was too ashamed about this prison thing, anyway. He didn't speak again till they reached the outskirts
of Landerley.

Raven viewed the limestone houses beneath the big live
oak trees and the town square with cynical contempt.
"Doesn't look much different. Same narrow streets—same
narrow minds. Same big windows. Same big eyes watching everything you do. Same big-nosed snoops gossiping
about everything you do. Same big liars. Reminds me of
prison."

"Not much has changed."

"Not much but me. I've lost my tolerance for back-
stabbing gossips and liars."

"So, what do you want to do on your first day back?"

"I reckon you know. I want to find *her* and start evening the score."

"You'd better stay out of trouble."

"Lula said she heard Innocence has been planning to
hightail it to San Francisco as soon as my pardon came
through."

Doug said nothing.

"So, has she?"

"Damn it, Raven. Forget her."

"If you don't tell me, I'll just ask around. Then the
whole town'll know I'm out to find her."

"I saw her in Dripping Falls yesterday, grocery shopping for her mother. So maybe Innocence is still here, seeing after her."

"She'd better be. But if she isn't, I'll just follow her to San Francisco."

"Why don't you do the smart thing and stay the hell away from her? She got you out."

"With a pardon. Which means I'm pardoned for a crime. I didn't commit a crime. Maybe I shouldn't care about that little technicality. Just like I shouldn't care that I lost two years and everything else I ever did care about— like a small fortune in real estate, my name and my self-respect."

"That's right. Maybe you should start concentrating on your future."

"Some things are mighty, mighty hard to forget. I figure *she* owes me plenty."

"I'm not saying forget. I'm saying go on. Choose a new woman."

"I've got a record now. What woman would want me?"

"You were innocent."

"Now there's one helluva tricky word. Prison leaves a dirty mark. The less stained your shirt when you go in, the dirtier the mark seems to you when you get out. I learned about the dark side of my soul. We've all got one. The coldness inside me is so terrible I don't know if I can ever feel alive again."

"You need to go forward. Not dwell on—"

"The past has a way of catching up to you, if you don't deal with it. I ran once. I'm not running again. I've got to find whoever killed Pam, whoever tried to pin it on me. How can I do that, if I don't find out what Innocence knows?"

"You can be kind of rough on people . . . sometimes."

Raven's mouth thinned. "People have been kind of rough on me. She has it coming."

"Maybe . . . you should go easy on her. I mean, she had a kid and two puppies with her in the grocery store. Did she tell you about her little girl?"

Raven missed the careful note in Doug's question. He was thinking instead of how strange it was to hear she'd given birth to a child when her beautiful body hadn't been blemished by a single stretch mark. Just the thought of her naked made him heat up and ache with frustrated male needs. Prison could starve a man for a woman. Quickly he told himself it wasn't her in particular he wanted—any female would do.

"You know, Raven, this kid of hers reminds me—"

"If you're thinking to soften me up, stop. I don't give a damn about her kid or about anything else but evening the score."

Doug was silent.

Out of the corner of his eye Raven caught a glimpse of red hair across the square, of a slim woman in white with a long graceful neck. Only one woman he knew had hair that color and wore it in an ugly, little bun.

Funny—Innocence coming into Landerley the same day he got out of prison. Maybe she was looking for him, too.

She was dressed in white silk—again.

Raven braked so abruptly their shoulder harnesses locked. "Speak of the devil. Or in this case, his prize witch."

Innocence and her sister were stepping out of Judith Lescuer's Cadillac which they had parked conspicuously in front of Landerley's only drugstore. Linda went into the hardware store and Innocence into the pharmacy.

"Keep driving, Raven."

Raven parked on the opposite side of the street. "End of the line, Doug."

"Don't do anything stupid."

"You're my friend, not my keeper. God knows, I've had enough keepers to do me a spell. As I told you before, I don't want any more."

Both men got out and angrily slammed their doors.

"Would you mind picking up an ax and a chain saw and a few other things while I go into the pharmacy?"

Doug nodded grimly, and then Raven handed him a list and some cash. As they started across the street, Raven was aware of hidden eyes behind the big windows. He hated feeling so self-conscious, as if people were thinking him a lesser man than he'd been before prison. Maybe he was. Prison hadn't exactly brought out the finer qualities in his character. Instead he'd picked up a lot of pointers on how to bully, intimidate and brutalize. Revenge had festered in his heart for two long years. He felt darker, colder and lonelier—unbearably lonely. They said he had blood on his hands; maybe he did.

Raven had discovered he was as low and base and as tough as any inmate there, that he'd do anything to survive. It didn't help his battered ego that besides the stigma of prison he was dead broke from legal fees and the neglect of what was left of his properties. He didn't know how he was ever going to get started again.

Even so, he held his head up as he crossed the street with Doug. When he saw a woman snap her little boy out of his path and hurry him away, Raven felt cut to the quick. But he forced a smile and said hello to the kid, which frightened the mother even more. When her little boy smiled back, she yanked his hand harder and rushed him away.

Raven flushed darkly. "See that? Decent people are afraid of me now, Doug. If Innocence had come forward immediately, I might have found Pam's killer by now and cleared my name. At the very least, Innocence cost me two years. And I intend to make her pay."

He spoke before he saw the tall man with the wide belt and silver belt buckle that matched his hair striding toward them and realized he was Sheriff Orley.

Raven resented the broad hand the sheriff laid authoritatively upon his shoulder. Too many guards had laid their hands on him.

"I'd lay low, if I was you, pardner," the sheriff said in a slightly bullying way.

"Well, you ain't me—pardner," Raven replied, ducking underneath the sheriff's arm and adjusting his black Stetson to a jauntier angle as he headed into the pharmacy.

Nine

Gooseflesh crawled all over Innocence the second the door of the drugstore was thrown open, and she felt the subtle power of the tall broad-shouldered figure that stepped inside. *He* just stood there stabbing a hand through his thick, curly black hair, adjusting his Stetson and letting the door bang behind him so jarringly every item on every shelf in the store shook. Especially her.

Raven's hard, ice-hot eyes swept the store, zeroing in on her, assessing her with predatory interest. She went hot and then cold. It was suddenly difficult to remember why she'd thought it smart to deliberately seek him out today.

Well, it had seemed the right move at the time.

Because she had decided Raven White was the kind of trouble it was no use to run from. If she went back to California before this thing between her and Raven was settled, then it would only be a matter of time before he came after her. And if she wasn't here, he'd probably make things worse between her and her family. Things were bad enough as it was. Judith and Innocence were barely on speaking terms.

Her mother had been furious that Innocence had admitted she was the hitchhiker; she'd grown angrier when Innocence had fought to get him out of prison, angrier still when Innocence started getting threatening phone calls. Innocence was angry at her mother, too.

"How can you side with him?" Judith had demanded.

"I had to tell the truth, Mother."

"The truth is he seduced you," Judith insisted.

"It was more a mutual thing."

"You were vulnerable—because of Timmy."

"Because of you, Mother."

Innocence had blown it, then. Her mother liked to lay the blame on others. Never on herself.

Raven picked up a sports magazine that featured leggy models in bathing suits and thumbed through it, glancing up from time to time, his expression dark and mocking, as if he were comparing her to the models.

Her eyes widened when he grew bored with the magazine and rolled it up. His gaze swept her body. Then he strode toward her.

Innocence wanted to run, but he blocked her only escape.

She tried to calm herself with the thought that she would reason with him, that he would not dare mistreat her in a public place.

Still, her pulse thudded harder every time his boot heel resounded on the wooden floor.

In his white starched shirt, jeans and boots, he seemed dangerously powerful, very much the primitive male. For a numbed moment she could only stare as a warm flush of excitement ran through her.

She barely heard what the pharmacist was saying about the pain medication the doctor had suggested Judith try, since her mother kept complaining that the others didn't work.

The pharmacist broke off in midsentence when Raven set down his magazine and leaned his tall, muscular body negligently against the counter and looked at Innocence, a cynical grin on his lean, handsome face.

Her pulse raced when he tipped the brim of his black hat back. His hair was black and glossy under the lights. She saw the deep lines around his eyes and mouth that had not been there before prison. There seemed a new hardness to every feature. His smoldering eyes were narrowed, his sensual smile grimmer, his husky voice taut.

"Don't let me bother you," he said, too politely. "Go right on doing... whatever it is you're doing."

Innocence lowered her lashes and fought to concentrate on the prescription she was writing, but her pad blurred. Her signature came out a scribble.

"Maybe you should sign yourself *Sweet Hitchhiker*, the way you did when you came to visit me in prison," he taunted. "I didn't have any trouble reading that."

"That's not my name!"

"That's how I always remember you, though," he said in that smooth, hard tone.

In spite of his grin, his features were so cold and stark they froze her.

She knew he hated her for the wrong he imagined she'd done. There were those who had warned her that he was evil, that he would never appreciate the fact that she had worked very hard to free him. They had assured her that her only recourse was to run.

"Look, I told you how sorry I was," she whispered.

He stared coldly at the base of her throat and then at her breasts. "Right," he muttered in a thick, odd voice. "So, you did. And like I told you before—sorry doesn't do much good. And you are lucky I'm a forgiving man."

He said no more. The awkward silence that followed was finally broken when the pharmacist cleared his throat and began to count tiny pills into a brown bottle. "Is there something I can help you with . . . Mr. White?"

Raven's chilling green gaze fell from her to the leggy model on the cover of his magazine and then insolently back up Innocence's body and face. "Thanks, but I've found what I'm looking for."

With shaking hands, Innocence took the bottle of pills from the pharmacist.

Raven grabbed a small box from a nearby shelf and slapped it on top of his magazine. "On second thought, this might come in handy," came his velvet taunt. With a fingertip he traced the naked leg of the model on the cover.

Lowering her eyes, Innocence looked down at his purchase. Her senses catapulted as she remembered the little box and the wrapper that had been on the bedside table in the motel the morning after they'd made love. It was on the tip of her tongue to lash out that the brand was no good. But she caught herself.

Raven cocked his head back, his curious green gaze having caught her look of alarm. "You were about to say—"

She bit her tongue. "Oh—nothing."

"Thought I'd better buy some. Just in case I get lucky my first night of . . . freedom."

As the pharmacist's eyes went from Raven to her, Innocence felt a searing sensation of degradation.

A single tear burned a path down Innocence's white face. She whirled away. The little bottle she'd been holding went flying, scattering her mother's pills everywhere.

"Oh, dear— See what you made me do!" Feeling wretchedly humiliated, Innocence sank to her knees, brushed at the tears dampening her lashes and began frantically picking up pills. But her hands shook so badly, she kept dropping them.

The pharmacist called another salesperson to ring up Raven's purchase while he helped Innocence retrieve the pills.

Two of the pills had rolled almost to the toes of Raven's black boots. He stared down at them and then at Innocence who was weeping softly, obviously too afraid to come near him. Despising himself for the sympathy he felt toward her, he slowly sank to his knees, picked the two pills up, and reaching for her hand, placed them in it. Her shaking fingers felt like ice.

Then her fist closed defiantly. *"Why don't you just go?"* she whispered. "Haven't you embarrassed me enough?"

"Oh, not nearly enough," he murmured, his voice tight. "I'm just warming up."

He stood up again, and as Innocence crawled about the floor searching for the rest of the pills, she was aware of Raven watching her as he counted out his change, paying for his embarrassing purchase with nickels and pennies so the sale would take the maximum length of time. Thus, he was still digging in his pocket for three pennies when she stood up again with her pills.

Plunking the last pennies down on the counter, his hand brushed hers as if by accident. At the jolt of his touch, she jumped away.

He smiled. "I'm surprised and . . . flattered you didn't skip town." He picked up his package.

"Don't be!"

"I kinda figure you stayed to see me."

"If I did, it was to tell you that just because I got you out of prison doesn't mean that we—"

"Surely you're not going to break my heart in front of these nice people and tell me it's over between us," he murmured in a falsely hurt tone. "And just when I thought my luck was starting to turn."

"You know perfectly well it was over after that first night—"

Mr. Sanders, the pop-eyed pharmacist and his sales-clerk were hanging on every word.

Innocence blushed. No doubt they'd be on the phone to everybody in town as soon as she walked out the door.

Without another word Innocence paid for her pills and raced past Raven toward the door, praying that somehow she could reach her car and drive away before he caught her.

But Raven got there first, springing lithely in front of her before she could open her door. He leaned as negligently against her car as he had against the counter—as if he had all the time in the world to torment her.

"Did you have to be so beastly in there?"

"Maybe it's all I know how to be now."

Innocence shrank from him. "Please . . . please, why can't you just lay off and let me go?"

His face grew so dark and hard she was afraid of what he might do right there in front of the whole town.

"If you're that scared of me, why did you get me out?"

"Because it was the right thing to do," she whispered.

His cutting gaze slashed her. "And you're the kind of girl who always does the right thing?"

"I try to."

"You picked me up. You went to bed with me. I was a stranger. Did you think that was so right—"

Revulsion at his interpretation of her own actions flared in her eyes, and because he thought it was revulsion for him, his face hardened.

"No... It was the worst mistake of my life. I'm sorry that I went to bed with you. Sorrier than you'll ever know. Sorry I ever met you." There were tears in her eyes, in her voice.

She flinched when his hand grasped her upper arm angrily. He dragged her to him. "Not nearly as sorry as I am," he rasped in a low, fury-filled voice. "But I would have come forward for you."

"I *did* come forward for you," she whispered.

"The hell you say."

The thinness of her silk sleeve was scant protection against his searing, viselike grip. Her senses registered how hard and powerful he was, and she began to shake with horror at the realization that she longed for him to hold her, to touch her—to forgive her. To do more.

Dear God.

Doubling her hands into fists she began hammering at him with her fists, but her weak blows had no effect against that thick wall of muscle and bone.

"Let me go!" she hissed, even as she felt terrified by the crazy, ever-intensifying urge that tempted her to quit fighting and move into his hard body instead of away from it, that tempted her to reach up and gently stroke his rough cheek and run her fingers through his crisp, curling black hair. If he had said so much as one kind word, she would have sunk to her knees and kissed his feet and begged for his forgiveness.

But he didn't.

And because she hurt so much, she spat hateful cruel words instead. "I can't stand for you to touch me!"

He dropped his hands abruptly. His green eyes were ice.

"I did come forward—as soon as I knew," she whispered. "But that doesn't mean I want someone as low as you pawing me."

His beautiful mouth curled into a sneer. "You were two years too late."

"As I said—I didn't know."

"And I say that's not good enough."

"Look, I feel terrible about it. But why don't you just leave me alone? I didn't plan to see you again after that night. I didn't want to." Just for an instant she remembered the vivid sweetness of his heated passion. She remembered that only in his arms had she learned what love was. Quickly she brushed aside the tantalizing memories and aching needs. "We said no strings."

His face twisted. "Damn you. There are strings, honey. Lots of them. More than I ever imagined there could be between strangers." Something in his low, passionate voice made her shudder. "Pam's dead," he whispered. "And . . . you're going to lead me to her killer. You're going to help me clear my name."

"I didn't have anything to do with that."

"Maybe. Maybe not. Maybe you were just in the wrong place at the wrong time, but you damn sure had plenty to do with me going to prison. You were my alibi, and you vanished."

"Well, you're out now. Free."

"Am I? You have a funny idea of freedom. I lost everything—defending my case and then losing it, appealing it. Because of you I lost all my money, my friends, my name—hope. Even my soul. I figure you owe me plenty."

"I've done all I can."

"Oh, no you haven't, honey. Not by a long shot."

"What do you want?"

"For the two years I lost, I want two years of your life."

"I have a new life." She held up her left hand.

Raven's mouth curled cruelly as he studied the large diamond Matthew had given her. "Yeah, but not with him."

"What are you saying?"

"You belong to me now, honey."

"You're crazy," she gasped.

"Yeah." He grinned darkly. "That's what they all said in prison. But, you want to know something funny? Even when I hated you the most in that foul, stinking cell, I remembered how good you were in bed. I've decided that if I let you go, I'd be punishing myself. That's why I'm going to let you work off your debt."

"That is the most outrageous, the most insulting..." Her hand lashed toward his face, but he grabbed it. Too late she remembered his reputation for violence and realized that such violence invited like violence from him.

Her breath caught as his grip tightened on her wrist and he pulled her closer. "Careful," he murmured. "People are watching. You wouldn't want them to think we're having a lovers' quarrel."

"But you would. You want them to think we are lovers. That's why you did what you did in the drugstore. That's why you followed me out here. You want them to think I'm going to climb back in your bed."

His face took on a cold, seductive quality that both repelled and attracted her. "You are."

"No—" But even as she protested, she swayed closer to him.

"I own you now."

"Never!"

His glittering gaze held her prisoner even as every instinct told her to flee. "Why not? Honey, you've owned me since the day I met you."

"You can't just harass me for no reason."

His warm breath fanned her cheeks. "I've got reason. Two lost years of my life. Then there's Pam. And Noah Rose."

Her frightened glance fell to Raven's sensual mouth, to the mouth that had once kissed her with such gentle reverence.

"Noah who?" she whispered.

"Pam's old boyfriend. Maybe yours as well."

"No!"

Raven's own gaze was ravaging the parting softness of her lips too, as if he found it as difficult as she did to concentrate on their conversation. "Honey, the reason Frank and I gave Pam a job was because we knew she was running from this guy and we wanted to protect her. She said Noah wouldn't let her alone." He paused. "I have a weakness for women in trouble. That's why I stopped for you that day. I would never have hurt Pam."

Innocence licked her suddenly dry lips with her tongue. "I...I know that." For an instant, despite everything, she felt again that deep, dark desire inside her, devouring her will to resist him.

When he pulled her closer, she forced herself to try to twist free. But he used his superior strength and easily crushed her against the car. One of his long, oak-solid thighs insinuated itself between her legs. She could feel his heart thundering, but no faster than her own. Wildly she wrestled to free herself, but every movement made him breathe harder, made his grip burn tighter.

"Be still," he growled.

She stopped struggling abruptly. "Let me go," she pleaded softly.

For another long moment he held her. Then one of his hands moved to the nape of her neck and gently brushed the silken tendrils of hair that fell there. Her heart fluttered wildly. She swallowed a soft moan.

Satisfied, he removed his hands, and slowly eased his body from hers.

"Don't try to run," he warned.

She nodded.

"After we gave Pam that job," he muttered, picking up the thread of their conversation, "she still stayed scared all the time. She wanted to know where Frank and I were every second— She was scared Noah would find her, and she didn't want to be alone any more than she had to be. The day I picked you up at Scud's Crossing, Noah drove by. I figured out while I was in prison that he must have been the one who drove off and left you."

"No! I never heard of him," Innocence said. "I don't know him. It was my mother who drove off."

"If you're lying, I'll find out, and I'll make you very very sorry."

She willed herself to snap out some hateful barb, but she was too rattled to think of one. His steel arms came around her. She was ashamed when another ember of unwanted desire flickered hotly to life. Frantically she fought to push him away.

Her look of disgust caused Raven to writhe inside. He released her abruptly.

She made a strangled sound as she fell back against the car. "Surely you didn't mean what you said about wanting to own me."

"I did. And I will." But his voice was unsteady as he opened the door for her.

She didn't question why he was letting her go. "Do you really think I'm going to be your punching bag till you work all the anger out of your system?"

"Something like that."

"Go to hell."

"No way. I've already done enough time there because of you." He crinkled his package. "What I'm looking forward to tonight is a little piece of heaven."

Her cheeks burned. "You crude, conceited . . ."

"Beast?" he finished with dryly. His slow, mocking grin flashed. "Whatever I am, I owe it all to you. So what do you say—yes or no?"

She got in her car and slammed the door.

"I'll be across the street in Panjo's if you change your mind." His husky voice was disturbingly soft.

She fumbled frantically for her keys.

"I could do with a beer." He leaned into the car, his darkly lashed eyes on her lips again. "But I'd rather have a woman." His cold face was flushed with desire. "I seem to remember you taste a lot sweeter than beer."

"You hate me," she whispered.

"But I want you, too."

"You won't have any trouble picking up a woman in Panjo's."

"You've got that right."

She started the car.

"I'd rather have you," he murmured.

"No."

"Maybe later," he jeered in that low, velvet tone even as he pushed himself away from the car almost savagely. "Anytime. I'll be waiting."

Vitally male, his power and determination were carved in his features for all the world to see.

"Never!" she snapped.

Ten

The huge hot pink neon sign above Panjo's blinked on and off against the fiery sky.

Innocence had said never to Raven White. She had vowed never to the secret desire in her own heart.

But never was never so short.

Never had been no longer than it took her to rush Linda back to the ranch, remove Matthew's ring, and change hurriedly into a wispy, red silk sundress and jacket and then race back to town.

Innocence swerved recklessly from the bridge onto the square. The slanting sun seemed brighter and hotter than it had at noon. Harsh red rays glinted through the cypress trees. A warm wind was blowing the thin leaves of those tall trees. Long tangled black shadows fell across the limestone walls of the bar.

Innocence grabbed her scarf and got out of the Cadillac and climbed the stone stairs to Panjo's only to lose her nerve when she heard the faint sound of that song she had played so many times when Raven had taken her dancing before.

"Wildness." The heavy beat pulsed in her blood.

Was Raven playing it? Was he dancing with somebody else? At the thought a funny little band of pain seemed to circle her heart.

If you're smart you'll leave him alone.

Innocence placed her hand on the unvarnished door.

Where did smart ever get me?

Defiantly Innocence pushed open the thick door. The throbbing music grew louder, the rhythm and crooning melody swirled around her. She remembered the night when Raven had held her so tightly and they had danced for hours. He had not been a good dancer, but never had she enjoyed dancing more. Never had she danced with any man and been so aware of every place where his flesh joined hers, however lightly; never so aware of a hand at the small of her back, of long tapered fingers warmly wrapping around hers, of hot, sleek male muscle and bone mashing against her breasts and belly. She hadn't cared that he'd been clumsy at first and stepped on her feet. She hadn't minded leading him or teaching him. And he'd repaid the favor in spades—leading her and teaching her later, when he'd bedded her.

The song ended.

Some hidden hand played it again. There were smothered groans of protest, but no one dared do anything about it.

When Innocence stepped deeper into that smoky blackness, a dozen pairs of male eyes from a nearby table riveted to her. A big brown hand lifted a beer mug in a friendly salute. A slurred voice rang after her boldly. "Hey Red, why don't you join us? We'll buy you a drink?"

Tension knotted her stomach as she scanned the room for Raven and found he wasn't there.

Her bearded admirer got up so fast his chair crashed to the floor. She pivoted away from him, but not quickly enough. His sweaty hand clamped down on her shoulder. "I said I'd buy you a drink!" He pulled her close and she felt his hot, beery breath against her cheek.

"Can a lady say no?"

"Ladies in red never do."

All the men at the table guffawed.

The brute's hand tightened dangerously. Then he started to drag her toward his table as if she were some toy for his pleasure and not a human being. When she twisted to free herself, she felt a spaghetti strap pop loose under her jacket. She cried out.

In the next instant Doug had materialized out of the darkness. The man's rough fingers were gone and she was free.

"Sorry Bruce, she's with me," Doug growled pleasantly as he put a proprietary arm around her and led her away from the rowdy group toward the bar.

"Thanks," she whispered.

Beneath the faint neon light of a beer sign, Doug's blond hair gleamed white and his grim blue eyes were colorless. In a lower tone he murmured, "What kind of crazy stunt do you think you're pulling—coming in here? Dressed like that?"

"I'm looking for Raven."

"If you're smart you'll leave him be—at least for tonight. He's a lot more dangerous than Bruce."

"You sound like one of the little voices buzzing inside my head."

"You'd better listen to this one, girl."

"You were the one who got me to help him in the first place."

"I came on pretty strong that day. Your mother had driven us all mighty crazy before you came. But I've figured out you aren't what I thought you were, what Raven had led me to believe you were. You're sweet—"

She touched his sleeve. "You're sweet, too, Doug." She sighed. "Where is he?"

"In the back room playing pool. But go home, sweetheart. Give him a day or two. Give *me* a day or two to calm him down."

"I can't do that, Doug."

"He's been nursing a grudge against you for two long years. The hate's been growing inside him like explosive gas. And tonight he's been trying to drown the hate. He's been drinking real steady ever since he came in here."

"I've been thinking about him pretty steady, too, since I last saw him. Buy me a drink, Doug and I'll join him."

"Honey, he hasn't had a drink in a long time. He's not holding it like he used to. He hasn't had a woman, either. When he sees you in that dress, he's liable to do anything."

"Don't you understand, Doug? I've got to settle this thing between Raven and me. I can't go forward with my life any more than he can, till I do. I'm all mixed up, Doug. I don't know who I am or where I'm going anymore."

"What happened to him isn't your fault."

"But he thinks it is."

"Leave him alone."

"I wish I could."

How could she tell him that it wasn't only guilt that had brought her here? How could she tell him that the thought of Raven looking for another woman tonight had been

more than she could bear—when she could hardly admit
it to herself?

"You're as crazy as he is. You know that, don't you?"

She nodded, and he ordered her a beer.

"What about your... little girl?" he asked.

"She's with Marcie and Linda."

"That's not what I meant."

Innocence couldn't think about Ashley. "Don't ask so
many questions. I'm all out of answers, Doug. I used to
think I was smart. But I don't know anything tonight except that whatever Raven's become, he thinks I'm to
blame. And maybe he's right. He's hurting. And because
he is, so am I."

Raven swayed silently as he leaned low over the table at
the far end of the room and sighted down the length of his
pool cue. Pushing the brim of his black hat higher on his
forehead, he squinted, trying to focus, but the cluster of
bright balls just grew blurrier against the fuzzy green felt.

*Instead of the balls he saw her face. The face he had
been trying to exorcise from his tortured brain all night.
Her big brown vulnerable eyes. Her frothy red hair. Her
long, slim neck. Her breasts.*

He was free. He could have what he wanted now.

The hell he was free.

The wanton vision of delectable femininity blurred.

But not before his hands had begun to shake. He was
way too intoxicated to keep up this farce that he was playing pool. The hateful fever that had burned in his blood
when he'd watched Innocence drive away had only flamed
hotter with every beer he'd drunk. His craven need was
stronger than anger, stronger than pain, stronger even than
revenge; it was a driving force that threatened to consume
him from the inside. Doug was acting as nervous as a green

boot, and he kept checking on him every half hour or so, trying to talk him into going home.

But Raven couldn't face going home alone tonight.

He needed a woman. He needed one badly. Maybe then he could forget *her.*

Then why hadn't he found one?

Because of her.

Because even more than he wanted to forget her, he wanted her.

He should never have let her drive away.

When the half doors to the pool room swung open and a slim girl moved hesitantly inside, Raven didn't glance up even though instinctively he knew she was a woman. Not till he heard a low wolf whistle and a "Hey, get a load of that dish in red."

And when he did Raven stared wordlessly, his eyes blazing as hotly as bonfires.

Innocence had come to him.

He felt a savage satisfaction; then a fierce fury at the intensity of the emotion her mere presence ignited.

But there was no denying his burning hunger as his gaze roved the length of her slim form, from the top of that coppery knot down the length of her slender neck, to linger on her lush breasts, too much of which were exposed by the low-cut jacket of her red minidress.

Months of unhappy, pent-up longing surged through him as he studied those long curved legs and red high heels.

Across the smoky, shadowy room, her gentle eyes scanned the other men's faces until she found him.

She blushed uncertainly, guiltily. Then she smiled, and the sweetness of it cut through him like a knife. Innocence and wildness—the same tantalizing mixture that had attracted him before lured him now. It was all he could do to control the violent urgency of his fierce need.

He wanted to go to her. To forget what she had done. He remembered how he'd felt as a child, craving warmth and love, hugs and kisses from his mother. This woman brought back those old longings, only now they were stronger; only now he felt needier.

He forced himself to remember Pam's murder and the long months in prison. Innocence was no angel. She was Judith Lescuer's daughter. Cold anger coiled around him as he reminded himself of Innocence's part in his fate. Clenching the pool cue more tightly, he leaned over the table and pretended to ignore her.

But his carefully planned shot went wild. Balls clicked loudly, exploding off one another. Not one found a pocket.

Behind him a man laughed. "Losing your touch?"

Innocence laughed, too, in that shy way that was somehow so bold.

Furious, aroused, Raven flushed and pretended to study the arrangement of balls on the table again. But they blurred and he was aware of her moving nervously toward the jukebox, her hips swaying in that tight skirt. He was darkly, jealously aware of the other men watching her, too, and he felt a murderous desire well up in him to destroy any and all who dared touch her.

He took deliberate aim and then swore under his breath when the second shot was even worse than the one before.

When "Wildness" stopped, the silence seemed louder and heavier than the music. Innocence held up a quarter, so that it reflected the neon light directly into his eyes, before she slowly inserted the coin. After the quiet, the throbbing music charged the hot darkness that separated them like a live current.

The men were looking at him, looking at her—noting she had played the same song they were all mightily sick of because he'd played it more than a dozen times himself.

Everybody in the room felt this thing going on between them.

Raven didn't like people reading him, knowing him.

But his heart was like a deck of cards thrown face up on a table. He felt naked, exposed, and there wasn't a damn thing he could do about it.

The men knew he wanted her.

She knew.

The heavy jungle beat of the music pounded through him. He looked up at her then, and she leaned back against the juke box and began to toy with the top button of her jacket. When it came undone, her fingers moved lower to the next pearl-tipped stud, down that sculpted red bodice, and he watched those talented fingertips, spellbound, as they undid one after the other in that slow, languid way that made his blood course through his arteries like liquid fire. He tilted his black head back and took another long pull from his beer bottle. But his eyes never left her.

She tipped her head back and slowly arched her slim body, so that the jacket slid halfway down her naked arms. Then she smiled at him while it hung there before easing it the rest of the way off and letting it fall to the floor.

He studied her in silence. A broken spaghetti strap dangled against her breast. He wondered how that had happened.

She was a witch. She held him spellbound.

Red silk, what little of it there was, hugged her body like a second skin. It revealed too much breast, too much leg, too much pale golden flesh.

He wanted to be wrapped in those arms. By those legs.

And if what she was doing wasn't wanton enough, she began to fiddle with her hair, pushing a strand out of her eyes. Then with a deft movement she took out the hairpins and let the whole silken mane of curls spill over her bare shoulders. The other red strap slid off her shoulder, and she didn't push it back.

She looked loose and wild—free—like she had when she'd been naked in his bed.

The last thing he wanted was to make a fool of himself in front of all the men. He leaned over the pool table and strove for control, but his hands were shaking so badly the next shot was worse than all the others. The eight ball flew off his table and rolled up toward the jukebox. She stopped the ball with the tip of a red satin toe and then laughed up at him as she gracefully sank to her knees. He watched those long fingers close around that smooth black ball. She rolled it back and forth in both hands.

Every other man was watching the movement of those hands, too.

And suddenly Raven couldn't stand it. He threw his pool cue to the floor. By the time she got to her feet, he was beside her.

"What the hell are you doing here? Dressed like that?" He fingered the broken strap.

She tossed the ball up and down, smiling, still teasing him. And quick as a teased cat, he pounced. He caught the ball in one hand and her wrist with the other.

"You invited me," she said. "Remember?"

The pupils in her eyes were dramatically dilated, so that only a ring of dark amber encircled them. Close up her body seemed even more sensuous in that tightly fitting red silk, her lips more luscious. Hell, every part of her was more luscious. And she knew what she was doing to him.

"What took you so long—coming over?" she asked huskily.

The silky sound of her low, exultant tone shivered down his spine.

The dangerous, two-faced, betraying little witch.

For two years he had wanted her. All night he'd drunk and played that damned song over and over until he was half-crazy because he craved her so much.

"I was playing pool," he muttered.

"Oh, really?" Her eyebrows arched saucily. "So that's what you call it." Her lashes fell. "You weren't doing too well."

In spite of himself he smiled. "It never was my favorite game."

"Maybe you're just not in the mood for it." Her warm, dark eyes seemed to caress him.

"Hey, careful . . . where you head with this."

She ignored his warning. "Or maybe you're just out of practice."

"I'm out of practice doing a lot of things."

"You want to dance?"

"I never was any good at that."

"I liked dancing with you."

"I'm more in the mood for what came later."

"Are you?" she whispered, smiling at him with soft excitement. Reaching up she cupped his face with her gentle hands, stroking his hard jawline with her light fingertips, tracing his cheek, touching his crisp black hair. "I've missed you, too."

Then she placed her red silk scarf around his neck and kissed him, not in the wild reckless way he expected, and maybe he wanted, but ever so tenderly, ever so sweetly full on the mouth.

And just for a second all the cold hate and black loneliness fell away from him and he was tender, too.

He bent and kissed her softly, opening her mouth with the pressure of his tongue. Then he gently caressed her long, slender neck and her creamy shoulders until he felt her quivering and trembling beneath his touch. The music swirled around them, taking them back to that long-ago night when they'd loved each other without the hate.

She was delicious—and he was starved. The long months of repressed hunger for her sent racing tremors of desire through him. How many nights had he lain on his bunk in that narrow cell and dreamed of her sweet mouth, of her tender breasts, of her long slim legs . . . of her glorious frothy hair. He wound his fingers through the wild, perfumed curls. He had ached for her.

And she knew it.

Weakly, eagerly Innocence clung to him as his hard arms gathered her against himself ever more tightly, as his lips kissed her ever more passionately, his tongue roaming possessively inside her mouth, tasting her, loving her.

And deep within her a fragile new hope was born. She sighed and unknowingly uttered part of her impossible dream aloud. "I love you. I never wanted to. But I do."

I love you.

And those three words that had driven him to leave so many other women who'd used them thinking to possess him, were a thousand times worse coming from her.

They clawed through him, the husky sounds more deadly than Snake's thrusting shank.

He was a little boy again craving one kind look from his beautiful famous mother. Craving those three words. . .just once.

The other women who had said them to him hadn't mattered. But Innocence mattered.

And because Raven wanted those words from Innocence, he hated them from her. Because he wanted them, he felt himself sliding into some fatal vortex. He knew if he didn't break this embrace, he would be held in thrall by her forever.

For her love, he would have done anything. He would even forget his cold hate and put aside his desire for revenge.

But she didn't love him.

No one had ever loved him.

Wild anger that she would be so deceitful tore through him. She probably knew how much he wanted it. She was probably secretly laughing at him because he was so weak, so easy, so vulnerable.

All of a sudden he remembered they were in a smoky bar and a dozen other men were watching them. They'd seen her come in and play him for the fool he was.

Damn her. With her sweet, yielding softness she could destroy him.

He hurled her away, his eyes icy with anger.

Her own lovely eyes opened with a hurt, startled look and then widened even farther as he knelt down roughly, grabbed her jacket, threw it into her hands and propelled her out of the crowded poolroom and bar without so much as a word.

"What's wrong?" she breathed, pretending, he thought, to feel concern for him as he hustled her out the door.

Outside in the cool darkness he shoved her against the wall. "Just what did you think you were doing in there... coming on to me like a... a common..."

"Don't say it," she whispered, drawing a deep anguished breath. "I didn't feel like that. I wasn't... It wasn't like that."

"It was. And you were."

"No." Her crestfallen face went crimson. She looked past him. There was no way she could tell him the truth and admit that she hadn't been able to bear the risk that he might turn to another woman. No way that she could admit what she felt for him was the most powerful thing she'd ever felt for any man. Not after the way he'd acted when she'd accidentally told him she loved him. Not when his face was set and grim and he was so determined to hate her.

She swallowed miserably. "You wouldn't believe me if told you."

"Why did you come in there?"

Her mind whirled. What perverse awful reason could she invent that he would believe? Suddenly she felt exhausted by the effort it would take to make up some lie for him. "You're not going to stop till you get whatever it is you want from me, are you?" she asked dully, fingering the red scarf she had looped around his neck.

He nodded silently, his eyes cold.

"Well, I figured if I came on to you tonight we could both get whatever it is you're determined to do to me done. And then we could get on with our lives."

His lips curved into a bitter smile. "So you can marry another man," he ground out harshly, the thought making him more furious than ever.

"You are impossible," she whispered.

"You made me that way."

"I told you I loved you because most men like to hear those words."

"I don't." Jealously he yanked her into his arms again, and his hard mouth came down bruisingly on hers. "The last thing I want is more lies."

For an instant her lips were as soft as before. With her scarf she pulled his head closer to hers and seemed to almost melt as lovingly against him as she had in the bar.

He felt himself sliding down that fatal slope again.

Fortunately she wrenched herself out of his grasp and saved him. "No," she pleaded.

All he said was, "Then let's get the hell out of here."

Eleven

"Slow down. We're here," Raven's command was harsh and cold.

It was the first thing he'd said since he'd thrown her the keys to his truck and ordered her to drive, saying he'd had too many beers to take the wheel.

A rabbit sprang in front of her headlights and she swerved to avoid it. The truck careened wildly toward a wall of cactus and scrub cedar lining a deep ditch.

His strong hand closed burningly over hers and guided the steering wheel as she braked.

"You're hell on machinery, woman," he muttered.

"It's just that you make me so nervous. I can't concentrate . . . I-I can't think when you're around."

"Hey, you didn't hit the rabbit, and you got us here."

Her frightened eyes left his face and scanned the darkness. "Where? Where are we, Raven?"

"As if you don't know."

She looked around wildly and turned back to him. "No, I don't! But I know I don't like it here. And you're acting so strange, so dark. You're scaring me, too."

His truck was parked on a little slope beneath the lonely patch of shadow under a huge live oak. Hills covered with scrub cedar and cactus loomed between them and the moon. Even inside the truck, Raven felt the eeriness and desolation of the place.

"Maybe I want to scare you," he said. "Maybe that's the only way I know how to get the truth out of you." He leaned across her and silently opened her door. Then he jumped out his side, loped around the front of the truck to hers, and helped her down.

The dark seemed to close in around them. He felt more vulnerable outside the truck—almost as if hidden eyes were watching them.

"I don't like it here," she whispered, sounding more afraid. "Please, take me somewhere else."

"Later," he growled. "First, there's something you have to see."

He led her down the tree-lined gravel road toward a ruined two-story house that loomed out of the pale gray light like a huge black specter.

"I'm not taking another step till you tell me where we are."

"This is Pam's house. As if you didn't know," he said quietly, leading her closer. "Someone... and I suspect it was Noah... shot her in the throat with my gun and then burned the house to the ground while you kept me busy in Austin that night."

The awful image of Pam lying dead hung in the air.

Moonlight had washed all color from Innocence's face. From his too.

"Raven—I didn't have anything to do with that. You have to believe me."

"Do I?" He kept forcing her closer to the house. "I was supposedly on my way to see her that day...when I stopped and picked you up. You see, Pam used every trick in the book to try to get me to date her. She was always picking fights with me over stuff that happened in the office. She was always acting scared of Noah because she knew I felt protective of her when she did that. She was a good secretary, but she was a lonely woman. I liked her, but at the same time, I resented all her games. She kept staging her quarrels with me so everybody in town would think I wasn't treating her right. She wanted them on her side. The day she died I was furious with her over something she'd pulled at Frank's funeral. That's why I put off seeing her, but if I'd gone to her house as I'd promised instead of picking you up, maybe she'd still be alive."

They had reached the sagging porch.

"Did you ever sleep with her, Raven?"

He led Innocence up the broken stairs. "She wanted me to," he said darkly. "There was one night when I almost—"

"Almost?"

When Raven flung the ruined door open, he felt Innocence, tugging against his hand, reluctant to follow him. He turned back to her. "I didn't sleep with her."

"Why not?"

"Do you really give a damn?"

"Yes."

Something in her gentle voice made him answer her with the truth. "Because I knew I couldn't ever love her. Maybe I can't love any woman. She was too vulnerable, too unstable. I didn't want to hurt her."

"Why do you say you can't love—"

"I told you before. I had a lousy childhood. My mother died when I was just a kid. My father hated me. After her death, I became involved with . . . an older woman only to discover she was just using me to get close to my wealthy father. She succeeded. My father threw me out, and I ended up here. If I was cynical about women then, prison just made me colder."

Innocence laid a sympathetic hand upon his shoulder.

"I didn't want to hurt Pam," he finished bitterly. "And I hate the thought of her dying the way she did, of any woman dying that way. Most of all I hate people thinking I could do something that that. I can't get it out of my mind that Pam was waiting trustingly for me that day, and that if she hadn't been expecting me, she might not have opened her door to that butcher."

The interior of the ruined house was blackened and dangerous. The roof was gone, as well as most of the rafters. The ceilings and walls had caved in. Only the stone chimney was still intact. A faint breeze stirred through the house. Raven heard some sound, but when he called out no one answered. He decided maybe it was only the wind in the dry leaves. Or maybe it was only his imagination working overtime.

A board creaked from somewhere within the blackened house, and again he had the strangest feeling that the house was haunted by some malevolent presence.

"Somebody is in there," he whispered. "You wait here."

But when he started inside to check, Innocence clung to him tightly and wouldn't let him go. "No, the floor's too dangerous. Raven, let's get out of here. I'm afraid of this place."

"Doug's been trying to sell it—but people don't like it out here any better than you do."

"It wasn't your fault, the way she died," Innocence said quietly as she pulled him off the porch.

"Everybody else thinks it was."

"They only think that because I didn't come forward. Raven, I would have . . . if I'd known. Please believe me."

He considered the passion in her earnest face. The warmth in her eyes was almost enough to crack the ice shield around his heart. It had been a long time since anyone had looked at him the way she was looking at him now. As if she felt truly terrible about what had happened to him. As if she wasn't afraid of him and thought he was worth something. As if she truly did care.

She had said she loved him earlier in the bar.

Because he still felt vulnerable, because he wanted to believe her so much, his jaw went rigid, and he lashed out. "Yes, they think I'm a monster—because of you."

"Raven, please, don't be like this. Not with me. I feel awful. I'm on your side."

She caught herself, and the silence between them was heavy and thick as she sighed in defeat and looked away. "It's no use," she said in a funny lost tone that tore through him. "It doesn't matter what I say. You'll always think the worst of me . . . just like my mother always does. Just like Matthew used to . . ." She broke off.

Raven scowled. He didn't like being compared to Judith or her ex-husband. *Was Innocence right? Was he doing to her what everybody had done to him?*

She seemed so sweet, so honest. "It was my fault too, in a way," he conceded at last. "If I'd taken Pam's fears more seriously, if I'd protected her—"

"You couldn't have known," Innocence said softly.

Her gentle words of comfort warmed him. "There were signs," he said tersely, coldly. "I ignored them. She said she was getting threatening phone calls."

"Let's go." Innocence pulled at his sleeve. "It's not going to do you any good to stay here and brood."

"It's not so easy to stop." He turned to Innocence. His face was pale and harsh in the gray light. He had to make her know the cold hate he felt. "Prison's a hard place, and the violence there got inside me," he muttered in a thick tone. "Maybe it was always in me...beneath the surface...."

"No."

"Maybe prison just brought it out. Maybe the decent citizens of Landerley sensed it when they believed so easily I killed Pam. I was always a loner."

Innocence brought her hand up to his cheek. "No. All they saw was the circumstantial evidence."

"They say I killed Snake, that I'm a killer now."

"Is that true?"

"I don't know. Sometimes I feel so hard and violent— so full of rage, I do want to hurt people. I thought I wanted to hurt you. What if I am like they say? My own lawyer thinks you should have left me behind bars. Even Doug's afraid I'll hurt you. And maybe I will."

Hesitantly she turned over the back of her hand and ran it across his ravaged face. Her skin felt light and warm. Her stroking was infinitely pleasant. For the life of him, he couldn't jerk away from the treacherous pleasure of her comforting touch.

It was she who pulled away. "Raven White, I know all about dark feelings and despair. All about incriminating circumstances. All about hating yourself and blaming yourself. All about those who are closest to you thinking the worst of you. All about loneliness. I've made terrible mistakes, too. Maybe that's why I'm not afraid of you."

"Maybe you should be. Maybe I'll always blame you for everything. Maybe I even hate you and all I'll ever want is to use you—as a tool for revenge."

"Then use me. I give you permission."

"What?"

Her soft guilt-stricken eyes dared him, tempted him. "Go ahead. Maybe I deserve it. Not for what you think I did to you, but for other things."

His gaze shifted to her gentle face. To her beautiful lips. To the warmth in her brilliant eyes.

The coldness inside him dissolved and he was lost to the violent need for her, which had little to do with revenge and everything to do with love...

In the next moment he forced her head back with his strong, calloused hands, and his lips burned hers in a deep and penetrating kiss.

And the hate he wanted to feel for her was extinguished by a much hotter flame.

The flame continued to burn brightly even after Raven released her and took her back to his truck, even after he'd lifted her up into the cab and she'd slid shakily behind the wheel, even when she started the truck and he directed her expertly through the confusing maze of narrow, shoulderless county roads that led to his house.

He didn't touch her again. Except for his tersely barked orders, he didn't speak. But she was aware of the ruthless set of his jaw, the savage determination of his manner. And the sexual awareness between them remained as hotly electric as when he'd kissed her.

The closer they got to his ranch, the more fiercely her pulse pounded. Though she didn't look away from the road, she was only dimly aware of the racing strip of asphalt, only dimly aware of her headlights bouncing off the flying walls of tall cedar that clumped thickly along the shoulder. The dark power of Raven's animal magnetism seemed to envelop her, devour her.

"We're here," he said at last, in a goaded undertone after she took the last turn too sharply. "It seemed like it took forever."

"To me, too," she whispered, trembling as his log-and-limestone cabin loomed out of the gray light.

Located on the corner of the Clark ranch that touched Lescuer land, his house was almost as wild and lonely and desolate and scary as Pam's had been. Shrubbery and wild grapevines grew up the stone walls, the thick vines climbing high over the windows and timbers. Chest-high grass, white in the moonlight, swayed softly in the faint wind. Dead trees that lined the drive stood out black and sheer, their bare tangled branches tearing the half light like claws.

But the place was no wilder than the hard man who ripped the keys from the ignition the minute she stopped and pitched them on the floorboard. Quickly he pulled her into his arms, unhooking her sundress, dragging the one good strap down her arm and kissing her naked breasts with wild, avid hunger.

She felt a white-hot rush of heat as he lifted her from the cab, letting her half-nude body glide burningly against the length of his.

He didn't speak. He caught her hands in one iron fist and stretched them above her head against the cab of the truck. Then he kissed her on the mouth, long and deep, until her hands came around his neck, until he and she were both shaking. Too weak to stand, they sank together to the rocky ground, their hot mouths fused still.

His need was fierce, all consuming. She knew she excited him, but this was different than before. His hunger had built for two long years. This time he took no time for

tenderness. There was only dark, searing need and angry
passion.

His hands, which had once touched her so gently, tore
through her silken hair. His fingers roamed greedily over
her body. "Innocence. Oh, God, Innocence. Every night
I've dreamed of this. Of you. And hated you—because I
wanted you."

"I wanted to forget you, too. But I couldn't."

Her senses were assaulted by the intoxicating mixture of
warmth from his body heat, the clean, musky male scent
of him, and the faint odor of beer and cigarette smoke that
clung to him.

With blazing eyes he picked her up and carried her
through the high grasses, up the sagging wooden stairs,
across loose boards that creaked and groaned underneath
his heavy tread. He swore when the door was jammed, and
he had to kick it open.

There was a sweet, decaying mustiness to the air inside
as he carried her through the living room to his bed.

Someone had put on fresh sheets. They smelled sweetly
of laundry soap, she thought, as he pushed her down on
the bed and then stood up again to hurriedly rip off his
clothes. Then, except for her red silk scarf dangling from
his neck, he was naked—and boldly, blatantly aroused.

A sadness filled her when she saw the tangle of scars that
ran from his muscular shoulder across his chest.

"Undress." His voice was quiet, and yet the command-
ing tone stirred her.

He looked so tall, so strong, so very masculine, with his
corded muscles, powerful frame and purple scars.

Impatiently she sat up and unfastened her dress the rest
of the way, liking the way his brilliant eyes burned hotter
as she slowly slid it off.

"Come to me. Touch me," he ordered. When she crawled across the bed and then hesitated, he took her hand and led it to his body.

Softly she ran her hands across the ridge of hard, coiled flesh at his shoulder. Then she kissed the swollen scar with her soft lips, as if to heal the deep wound that had been there.

She felt him swallow hard. "Don't—" he growled, because her tenderness was so sweet it scared him.

"Let me. Please." Gently her velvet mouth trailed the entire length of that vicious scar with infinite compassion. "I'm sorry," she whispered. "So sorry."

A tremor went through him at the warmth in her voice.

"Don't be," he whispered hoarsely. "It's over."

"I'm so glad you didn't die," she said.

Her lips lightly caressed the raised skin and sent waves of tingling fire through him.

"So am I."

He saw the faint silvery marks across her stomach, the marks of her pregnancy, which he had not noticed before, but when he tried to touch them as she had caressed his scars, she pulled away shyly, trying to shield them from his view with her hands.

"You are beautiful. Every part of you," he murmured.

"So are you," she whispered.

Then he fell down upon her, kissing her so hotly, so fiercely, so ardently she shivered. His roughened hands ran over her arms, her waist, to her thighs, and as his leg slid between them she arched her body to welcome him, her fingers reaching up and eagerly guiding him to her.

Almost as an afterthought he remembered to protect her and reached for the package he'd bought in town. Then he thrust into her, the heavy weight of his body pressing her into the mattress. His hands closed over her hips, lifting them so that she fitted him snugly and he could fill her more deeply.

"Yes," she murmured. "Yes." She let out little sighs of unadulterated feminine pleasure.

And at these gentle mewing sounds his need became so violent, he lost all control and shuddered deep inside her. But her desire burned as wildly as his and she clung, sighing desperately, as wave after wave of her own warm rapture engulfed her.

Then it was over.

Completely over.

He rolled off her, folded his hands beneath his head, and stared moodily up at the ceiling. A breeze stirred across her hot body and she shivered.

She studied his lean, hard profile and willed one kind word from him. If only he would wrap her in his arms and just hold her.

One sweet gesture would be enough.

Not one came.

His icy remoteness chilled her even more than the cool breeze wafting across her.

What had she done?

A terrible feeling of disillusionment and hurt crept inside her. This time had not been like the last. This time there had been anger and passion—so much passion—but no spiritual union. He despised her so much he wouldn't even speak to her.

What had she expected? He had said he hated her, that he only wanted to use her.

Suddenly the magnitude of what she had done hit her. Why had she given herself to this cold, brutal stranger— for the second time?

A hot tear rolled down her cheek and then another. She brushed at them wildly, but they kept falling.

Because of her mother's constant criticisms, she had grown up feeling guilty about everything. Only after Ashley's birth, and with the help of her therapist, had she learned to stop that self-destructive pattern.

Tonight, because she'd felt so terrible about Raven's imprisonment, because she blamed herself for her mother's silence, she had let herself fall back into her old self-destructive habits.

What had happened to Raven wasn't her fault. She didn't deserve punishment. She couldn't allow him or anyone else to ever punish her—ever again.

Flinging the sheet aside, Innocence started to get out of bed.

She had thought his mood so dark he was unaware of her, until his heavily muscled arm wrapped around her waist and drew her back. "We're not through."

"No..." she whispered and struggled, frantic to escape him even as he shoved her beneath him.

"You have a lot to learn about me," he said in a low, flat voice, "if you think that after two years once is enough."

He crushed her against his chest and she felt the hard hammering of his heart. She pushed wildly at his arms, straining to break his hold. But he subdued her easily.

He bent over and brushed his mouth against hers and discovered the tears that dampened her cheeks, the tightness of her lips, which refused to open to his.

"Was it so awful for you then?" he rasped, drawing back. "Do you think I'm a monster—the way everybody else does?"

A convulsive shudder ran through her. "Can I please just go now?" she pleaded, squeezing her eyes tightly shut. "You got what you wanted, didn't you—revenge?"

"Will you be all right?"

"Yes. If you leave me alone."

His restraining hands fell from her smooth flesh. "Then go," he ground out. "Go. Get out of my life. Go back to that rich wimp who divorced you. Marry him again. It's what you want. It's what I want too."

But it wasn't what he wanted.

Coldly furious, Raven tore her red silk scarf from his hot neck and tossed it toward her in disgust. "Don't forget this."

With a horrified little cry of fear, she watched it flutter to the floor. Then she gathered her clothes and fled, racing lightly out of his room and across his living room to escape. When the front door slammed, it jarred every nerve in his body.

And his house suddenly felt colder and very empty without her inside it; lonelier even than his prison cell.

What had he done?

Raven got out of bed and leaned down to pick up his jeans. Instead his fingers brushed perfumed silk. He brought the scarf to his lips and inhaled deeply of her fragrance.

Then he threw it down and pulled on his jeans and boots. He had made love to her because he wanted revenge. But the bleak, bitter despair that closed over his heart told him that the joke was on him.

All he could taste was the salt from her tears.

All he could feel was her final involuntary shudder of revulsion when he'd asked her if making love to him had been so awful.

Her running from him tonight was a thousand times worse than her running the first time, even when he'd stood accused of murder. Because the need he felt for her now was so much more profound.

He had wanted to believe that he only wanted to use her and hate her and be done with her. But it wasn't like that.

She'd felt too good to hate; too sweet to forget. Her kindness and passion had made him feel that maybe life had more good than bad to offer. It had made him think that with her at his side he wouldn't care that so many people believed he was bad. Maybe he was worth something after all.

He had been scared by these feelings and new longings. He'd lain in the darkness beside her, wanting to caress her and not daring to reach out.

There was no way he could blame her any longer for Pam, because he knew in his gut she wasn't part of the murder.

He remembered Innocence materializing out of the mist at Scud's Crossing, looking scared and innocent and then cocking her thumb at him. He saw her leading him onto that dance floor, coaxing him gently with her softly shining eyes. He saw her standing at the end of that long, dark tunnel in prison looking terrified to see him again and yet radiant, too. He saw her throwing herself between him and that guard like an avenging angel. He saw her in the pool room in that slinky red dress, coming on to him in front of all those men.

She had fought for him.

At great cost to herself, as no woman had ever fought for him.

She was the best friend he'd ever had.

And he'd treated her worse than he'd ever treated any woman.

What had he done?

He'd been wandering in darkness, crushed by loneliness—until she'd kissed his terrible scars and taken him into her arms. Sinking into her body tonight had been the closest thing to glory he'd every known.

Too late he realized what he'd known that first night—
that he wanted her forever. He wanted her, every part of
her, not just her body. He wanted her heart and mind and
soul. He wanted the wondrous glory of her love.

He had been so hateful he had probably made her hate
him forever.

He went to his darkened kitchen and poured himself an
icy glass of water and tried to think of some way to start
over. Then he looked through the open window and saw
her. She was sitting on his swing, her diminutive figure
hunched over, her face buried in her knotted fingers. She
was weeping—silently, hopelessly.

Because of him.

She couldn't possibly want him in any lasting way. He
had no money. Nothing to give her—nothing but the taint
of prison and his harsh lovemaking and the cold, dark
misery in his soul.

The kindest thing he could ever do was to let her go back
to her rich ex-husband and her life at the top of the world
as a neurosurgeon. But kindness wasn't in his nature. And
taking what he wanted was.

Silently Raven set his glass down and opened the front
door. She sat up, startled at the sound of his boots stalk-
ing across the creaky boards of the porch toward her.

Tentatively he sat down beside her on the swing and
scowled when she instantly scooted as far from him as
possible.

"You probably hate scenes like this," she said.

"I hate that I made you miserable."

"Why? I thought that's what you wanted."

"It was." He put his arms around her, hating it when she
tried to push him away. Hating it when she took a deep
breath and closed her eyes, as if she wished herself in another place with another man—with anyone but him.

Raven knew he should be gentle, but he had forgotten how. "Yes, I know what I want from you now—again and again," he whispered angrily. "You—your mouth, your body, all of you." His lips moved over her.

But she thought he meant merely to take her and use her again, and she stiffened against his iron grip and forceful kisses. "I want to go home. I don't want to ever see you again."

His arm went around her waist, molding her to him, and he bent her farther back against the swing so that his warm lips could devour her throat and breasts. "Move in with me."

Helplessly Innocence shook her head, and tears of frustration leaked out from beneath her closed lashes.

"So, you could punish me...forever and ever." She paused. "That's how my mother treated me when I was growing up. That's how my marriage was. That's how I lived all my life...until a year ago. I-I simply couldn't bear to move in with you...and go back to that," she said, pulling free. "It's over."

He didn't stop her when she got up and ran toward his truck.

Twelve

It was nearly three in the morning when Innocence hurriedly parked Raven's truck underneath the carport between her mother's tumbledown barn and the new guest house. Her mother would probably threaten another heart attack tomorrow morning when she saw it and realized Innocence had spent the night with him, but Innocence was far too upset herself to worry about the guilt trip her mother would lay on her.

It galled Innocence that she had let Raven bully her into feeling she'd deserved such punishment from him. How could she have fallen back into the old self-destructive pattern of her childhood and marriage? How could she have offered him her body, knowing all he wanted was revenge? Her stomach tightened when she thought of how he had lain so still afterward, coldly despising her.

A strangled sob caught in her throat. There was no way she could see him again. Even though she hated the torment and darkness in him and wanted to help him, she couldn't let him destroy her fragile feelings of self-worth. He would have to work out his life as she had worked out hers.

An inner voice pricked her conscience. *Whether you like it or not, he is the father of your child. Doesn't he deserve to know that before you walk out of his life forever?*

Innocence couldn't face the thought of telling him. There was no predicting how he'd react. He might assume certain rights; he might make demands.

She brushed away her tears and opened the door to the guest house as quietly as possible, so she wouldn't waken Marcie and Ashley. But just as she stepped inside, the phone began to ring. She dashed for it, idiotically wishing it would be Raven.

"I told you to stay away from White, but you didn't," a chilling male tone whispered. "Now you have to pay."

"No!" But she had begun to shake.

"You should never have let him out of prison."

"Look, who is—"

"Or let him take you to Pam's house."

"How do you know that?"

"You should not have slept with him again. You are as bad as Pam was. So, you have to die, too, just like she did. But not before I get a taste of you, too."

Dear God.

Innocence sank weakly against the wall. "I'm not going to see him ever again. I promise. Just leave me alone—Noah," she pleaded.

The line went dead.

She hung up the receiver and then picked it up again. More than anything she wanted to call Raven. She knew that if she told him about the call, no matter how he might hate her he would come.

Then she remembered how brutal he'd been, how determined he was to believe the worst of her, and forced herself to unplug the phone. She double bolted her front door and went into her bathroom to get ready for bed.

She turned on the shower and began to strip. Naked, she scrubbed off her makeup while she waited for the water to get hot. Then she leaned closer to the mirror to inspect her mouth, which was bruised and swollen from Raven's kisses. Instead of her face and body, she saw Raven's darkly glowing eyes when he'd stared at her as she'd removed her clothes. Her fingertips traced the faint stretch marks she had acquired after Ashley's birth.

Even despising her as Raven had, her body had not displeased him. He had been ravenous for her.

And despite his coldness afterward, she wanted him still. She longed for his strength, his toughness—for his courage. He wouldn't feel weak and afraid the way she had just because some kook threatened him over the phone.

But if she called Raven, he would want to use her in bed again.

She stepped into the shower and let the warm water flow over her. Putting her face to the nozzle, she stayed there too long.

As soon as she cut off the water, she heard Ashley crying.

Without bothering to dry herself, Innocence yanked her nightgown off the hook above the door and put it on. Then she pulled her robe on and rushed to her child.

Marcie was already beside the crib soothing her. But when Innocence came into the pink bedroom, Ashley stretched her arms toward her and cried pitifully.

"Mama . . . the puppies . . . Get puppies."

"She just had a bad dream," Marcie said.

"Puppies!" Ashley screamed. "They scared of the dark."

"They're in the barn, darling."

"I wanna pet 'em."

"They're safe and sound, all curled up in their big box with their mother—sleeping. The way you should be. Go back to bed and we'll go out and see them first thing in the morning."

"No, Mama! Bwackie cwying. Outside."

"She can't be. I was just out there and I didn't see her."

Just then a defiant paw scratched at the front door.

Ashley leapt out of her arms and rushed to the door, straining awkwardly to reach the doorknob. When Innocence opened it, a black lab puppy jumped on the toddler, almost knocking her down. Ashley laughed as Blackie, tail thumping, licked her face.

Ashley loved every minute of this sloppy affection. "Mama, can she sweep wif me?"

"No, darling, I'm going to take her back to her mother."

"Me, too?"

"No. Go back to bed with Marcie. I'll come kiss you in a minute."

Ashley clung to Blackie stubbornly and put her thumb in her mouth and sucked very hard—considering.

"Darling, it's very late, and you're very sleepy."

Ashley, who was very suggestible, blinked sleepily and did not resist when Marcie knelt to pick her up. As Marcie lifted the child Innocence grabbed Blackie and headed outside, but one look at the darkened barn made her reconsider. Innocence still felt uneasy because of the threatening call. She went back inside and replugged her phone. Still holding the puppy, she dialed Raven.

He answered gruffly, sleepily—but on the first ring.

Her heart thudded. At the sound of his deep baritone, she felt too dreadfully foolish to speak.

"Innocence? Is that you?" His drawl was less gruff, more alert, silkier.

"Yes."

"Are you as unhappy as I am—sleeping alone? Do you want me to come over?"

"Dear God, no!" Her cheeks flushed. "I should have known you are so conceited you would think—"

"Honey, what's wrong?"

She took a shivery breath. "Raven, I-I'm scar..." She caught herself, realizing he would probably take any invitation to come over the wrong way. "I mean no! Everything's just fine. I'm sorry I ever bothered you."

"Innocence—"

She panicked and slammed the phone down.

"Who was that?" Marcie asked.

"Oh, just a...a...er... Nobody important!" Innocence replied tightly, collaring the squirming Blackie more firmly. "I'm going to the barn now—all by myself. I'll just be a minute."

Outside she switched on the porch light, but the faint glow of light from the low-wattage bulb scarcely reached the edge of the drive, much less the barn.

Clouds obscured the moon, but even in the darkness she saw the big barn doors gaping half open.

She'd been too upset to notice if they were open when she'd come home. Ashley, no doubt, had made a late visit to see the puppies. Marcie must have forgotten to close them.

Innocence hurried across the gravel drive to the barn, but she hesitated in front of the doors. The barn seemed so dark. So huge. A cool wind whispered through the trees, stirring dry leaves and branches.

From inside a stall, a horse nickered softly. Whining nervously, Blackie tried to wriggle free. Black Dog, her mother, barked and jumped against the first stall, where she and her litter were confined.

If their stall door was closed, how could Blackie have gotten out?

"Black Dog?" Innocence called, as she peered fearfully into the darkness. Black Dog's friendly yelp welcomed her, and she didn't feel quite so alone. Or quite so afraid of the dark.

As Innocence tiptoed into the barn she caught the familiar penetrating scent of fresh hay and the stronger odor of manure. She was almost to the puppies' stall when she heard a stealthy sound behind her.

Innocence whirled just in time to see the doors slide shut behind her. Then the blackness seemed to swallow her.

She let Blackie down and said, "Who's there? Marcie? Raven?"

"It's just me!" came that dreadfully familiar male whisper.

Her caller.

"I believe we've spoken over the phone," he said mildly.

Hysteria bubbled up inside her. "Please—"

"Beg me. I like it. Pam begged, too."

Innocence, who had begun backing away from the voice, tripped over a bucket and collapsed clumsily into a bale of hay. She got up, her hands outstretched in the darkness as she blindly groped across the packed-earth floor toward the ladder that led to the loft, fumbling in the darkness for the rungs. Nothing had been stored in the loft for the past few years because Judith said it was too weak with rot and termites. Innocence scrambled up the rickety ladder anyway and then yanked the ladder up after her before the intruder reached it.

"Bitch!" he snarled when his big hands found only empty air.

There was another ladder at the far end of the loft. But maybe he didn't know.

She moved toward the center of the loft, and as she did a rotten board split. She jumped back right before it broke and crashed down into a stall.

The dogs whined.

The man laughed gleefully. "You can't get away from me. I know there's another ladder."

Innocence screamed and screamed when he made it to the other end of the barn and she heard the ladder groan under his weight. She couldn't stop screaming, even as she backed toward the dangerously weak center of the loft.

Her foot sank into rotten wood again, and this time she wasn't fast enough to spring to safety. The board gave under her weight. As she grabbed helplessly for a rafter, more boards splintered. Screaming, she tumbled head over heels to the ground.

Her head hit a wooden peg hung with tack. She felt another sickening dart of pain beneath her ribs when she struck the floor.

She lay on her back on the cold earth floor of the barn—too stunned to move, even when she felt the vibrations of the man's heavy footsteps coming ever nearer. He had climbed down the ladder. Dimly she was aware of him stopping. The next thing she saw was a huge figure towering over her with a raised pitchfork.

"I've got you now."

Outside the barn someone screamed her name.

As the pitchfork plunged down toward her face, she cried out desperately one last time as she lunged to one side.

The pitchfork jammed into the earthen floor. One prong split a board near her head; another snagged her hair.

She screamed when the man tore it out of her hair and lifted it again and took deadly aim.

There was a terrible rending sound from above them. A rafter groaned and then broke, and more of the sagging loft caved in on them.

There was a quick stab of pain.

Innocence uttered a final anguished scream.

Then all was terrifying blackness.

Raven's flashlight beam bobbed off tangled branches as he raced through thick cedar and crossed the slippery stone dam that bridged the ice-cold creek that separated the Clark ranch from Lescuer land. He slipped twice, not caring when he fell into the cold, clear water and got wet to his knees. He sprang back on the dam and made it to the other bank. Then he began to run again across the uneven, rocky pasture land, not caring when jagged boulders and cactus tore his jeans.

It was three quarters of a mile as the crow flies from his house across the creek and brush country to the Lescuer compound.

He made it in four minutes. Just in time to hear Innocence's terrified screams from the barn as the loft caved in beneath her weight. Just in time to hear more screams and then the crashing of more timbers from inside the barn.

He yelled her name, but her answer was faint, lost, dying away. Then there was terrifying silence.

The barn door banged open and a man tore out of it.

When Raven aimed his flashlight at him, the man rushed him and swung a pitchfork wildly. A prong struck the flashlight to the ground. Then the man jabbed at Raven's chest.

One blow swiped Raven across his bad shoulder, and he fell to the ground and rolled. Rocks tore his shirt and bit into his flesh while his attacker stabbed at him repeatedly. A booted toe kicked him in the stomach and knocked him breathless. A hand with a rock crashed hard against his temple. Vaguely Raven was aware of the pitchfork being raised again.

Lights came on at the main house.

There were shouts.

His attacker cursed and then jammed the fork down toward Raven. Raven lunged away and the pitchfork got only his shirt.

The man dropped the pitchfork and ran. Blood dripping down his brow, Raven grabbed the pitchfork and staggered slowly to his feet as the other man raced toward a car parked at the end of the drive. Raven wanted to go after him, but he was too worried about Innocence. She hadn't made a sound for a long time.

Raven threw down the pitchfork and picked up his flashlight. As he stumbled toward the barn, Linda ran up to him. He told her to call Sheriff Orley and an ambulance.

Inside the darkened barn Raven shouted for Innocence. All was dark and soundless except for the excited pawing and plaintive whining of a litter of puppies and their mother. When Raven unhooked their stall door, they scrambled awkwardly out of it.

He felt a growing desperation. "Innocence! Honey, please answer me."

A low, anguished moan came from the depths of the barn behind him. His flashlight danced along the walls of the stall. He whirled, shining the light down the length of the barn until he discovered the fallen debris from the loft.

He saw the mass of broken boards. The big black mother lab climbed on top of the boards and began to whine and bark loudly. Then she stopped to sniff excitedly.

When Raven shone his light on the dog, he saw the slim, limp fingers of a woman's hand sticking out from beneath a fallen board.

Panic tore through him as he clawed his way through the broken two-by-fours to the dog and the semiconscious woman.

Innocence moaned again.

Raven broke out in a cold sweat. There was so much stuff on top of her, she might be terribly injured and bleeding internally. But when he felt her wrist for her pulse, miraculously her heartbeat was steady and strong.

Carefully, slowly, he began heaving the boards aside until at last he had her free of them. She lay on the floor as still as death and yet more beautiful to him, in spite of the black smudges on her face, than ever before. He sank down beside her. After a long, silent moment, he gently began checking her neck and then every part of her body for broken bones.

"Innocence?"

Did he only imagine that her lips twisted in a gentle attempt to smile? She moaned pitifully again and then lay still, as if even that effort were too much.

When he carefully lifted her in his arms, her lolling head fell back and her red hair, which was matted with hay and splinters, streamed over his shoulders. She came to and moaned again, and every time she made that thin fragile sound it cut through him like a knife.

Then her slurred moans began to form intelligent syllables. But her voice was so faint, he had to strain to hear her.

"And I thought you had such gentle hands," she complained in that small, pain-filled voice.

"Honey, I'm trying to be gentle," he said tenderly.

"Try harder," she whispered.

"You're mighty bossy... like your mother."

"No...not like my mother." Her voice died and she lay still.

She wasn't like Judith. He knew that now.

Never had Innocence seemed so light, so fragile, as he clutched her limp body close to his heart and carried her toward the main ranch house.

If she died, he would die too.

If she lived, he had to find a way to make up for the way he had treated her.

Raven sat near the door, his muscular body hunched forward, his dark head bowed. He felt the most terrible remorse, as his large predatory-looking hands absently scratched Blackie.

Innocence, fully conscious now, was in a bedroom being examined by Old Doc Jamison while the ambulance attendants waited impatiently outside. Her babysitter had put her little girl to bed in the back of the house. The sheriff had come and gone. Frankly skeptical of Raven, Sheriff Orley had listened when Raven had explained his theory about Noah. Orley had reluctantly agreed to run a check on Noah.

Not that Judith hadn't tried to convince Orley that Raven was the guilty party. When Raven had asked Orley to leave some officers to protect Innocence, Orley had said he didn't have any to spare and that he was sure that if Noah was the culprit, he was probably a long way away by now.

When Judith emerged from Innocence's room, she was so thin and frail Raven almost felt sorry for her. Without makeup her pale, raw-boned face was haggard. He forced himself to remember it would be foolish to underestimate her.

Ignoring Raven, Judith spoke conspiratorially to Linda. "Doc Jamison's just about through," she said.

Raven sprang to his feet. "How is she?"

Judith lifted her nose in haughty disgust. "She'll live." Then she paused melodramatically. "As if you care."

"I do."

"Oh? Really? Then why have you done nothing but hurt her ever since you met her? I told her she was a fool to get you out of prison."

"That hardly comes as a surprise, Judith."

"A mother always has her children's best interests at heart."

"Then that explains why you dumped her out on the side of the road after her father died, and drove off so a villain like me could come along and take advantage of her."

"She attacked me that day! But that doesn't matter.... I have kindly chosen to forgive her. I'll always believe you came over here tonight, lured her out to the barn to seduce her and when she refused you you tried to kill her."

"I didn't need to seduce her," he said in a harsh, bitter voice. "She came to Panjo's looking for me."

"She's engaged to another man, do you hear me? She doesn't want to have anything to do with you."

"She came to me," Raven insisted, even though his guilt-stricken heart was wild with torment as he remembered how unhappily she'd run from him after his brutal lovemaking and coldness.

Innocence's bedroom door opened and Innocence limped slowly out of it, holding on to the wall, struggling to stand, looking white and weak in her soiled robe and diaphanous gown, and yet stronger than he would have believed. "Mother, please don't—"

Raven went to Innocence, and taking her slim hand he led her to a couch.

"What happened to your face?" Innocence asked, reaching up and gently touching the bloody gash at his temple, threading her fingers in his sticky dark hair. "Dear God . . . He tried to kill you, too."

He caught her hand. "I'm okay. But I want you to go to an emergency room—just to make sure you are."

"I won't have people seeing you two together. She's not going anywhere with you," Judith began.

"Oh, yes I am, Mother."

"The emergency room really is an excellent idea, Mrs. Lescuer," Dr. Jamison said smoothly.

"There's no telling what White'll do if you go off with him," Judith lashed out at her daughter. "He tried to kill you."

"He saved my life."

"That's a lie the scoundrel told everyone to protect his own hide," Judith said.

"Lying's your specialty, Judith, not mine," Raven muttered quietly as he put his arms around Innocence.

"I'm calling Matthew," Judith hissed.

"Mother, don't!"

Judith picked up the phone defiantly as Raven guided Innocence outside.

"I'll never forgive you if you make that call, Mother," Innocence whispered over her shoulder.

Then the door slammed behind them.

Judith went to the window and watched as Raven helped Innocence into his truck and then dismissed the ambulance attendants.

The touching scene was too much for Judith, who began to choke and cough when Raven got into his truck and pulled Innocence close.

Judith felt nauseated when Innocence laid her head upon the rogue's wide shoulder.

Judith wanted to gag as she watched the truck drive away.

She stared down the empty road for a long time, her heart fluttering painfully.

Innocence had actually threatened her not to call.

So what! Innocence had never made the smart move. She had become a doctor, when any smart woman would have married one and skipped all that hard, expensive school. Then she had married a rich man and kept working. She had neglected her husband, her child. Her *mother!*

If she let Innocence choose White, Judith would lose her forever.

Judith had never liked Matthew, but he seemed like Prince Charming compared to Raven White.

With the inspired melodramatic flourish of one who is in great maternal pain, Judith went to her desk and sank heavily into her chair. There she rummaged desperately through Linda's clutter for the address book that contained Matthew's unlisted number.

Raven stirred miserably on the hard cot, which was so narrow and short he felt like he was back in prison. For most of the night he'd lain wide awake staring at the ceiling, listening to Innocence's shallow breathing as she slept beside him in her larger hospital bed. Thus, the uncomfortable cot was not the only reason he couldn't sleep.

He was too aware of Innocence. More than anything he wanted to lie beside her, to hold her. And maybe because he couldn't, he'd begun to wonder if he would ever be able to sleep soundly again without having her warmly nestled against his body.

Innocence had tossed just as fitfully as he. The emergency-room doctors had found nothing alarming in her X-rays. They had held her overnight to observe her.

All night he had dwelled on the problems that were coming between him and this woman he was beginning to realize he could not live without. There was his hateful treatment of her for the past month. There was the cold way he had taken her to bed, his refusal to show her then how much he'd cared. There was her mother. There was Noah. Raven blamed himself for everything.

Raven kept ruminating about all these things, wishing she would wake up so that he could talk to her, when the telephone rang and she stirred.

It was still dark outside, too early for someone to call.

Drowsily she fumbled for the phone.

As if in slow motion Raven watched her lift the receiver from its cradle and press it against her ear. He watched her brows come together in alarm, her lips go white before she started to tremble.

Her frightened gaze flew to his face.

When she dropped the receiver, Raven lunged for it, but it crashed to the floor.

When he lifted it to his ear, all he got was a dial tone.

"Who was it?" Raven demanded.

Innocence sat up warily. Some of her color had come back, but there was still something in her frozen, controlled manner that aroused a deep fear in him.

"Ouch!" She flinched as she rubbed her bruised arms. "I feel like I've been in a boxing match."

Instantly Raven forgot about the caller and leapt to her side. One of his long fingers gently smoothed her tousled hair back from her bruised forehead. "You okay?"

She nodded, but her brave air of nonchalance was false. "I've got to get home...so I can get some rest. I-I haven't slept a wink here."

That was a lie.

"It's only six o'clock in the morning."

She threw back her sheets and winced again. "I want to go home. This place is too noisy. That phone call was the last straw."

"Not till your doctors release you," Raven said, his voice very hard, very male.

"Don't be ridiculous. I am a doctor."

"You're not in charge of this case."

"Why do you have to be so stubborn, Raven? I'm okay. I wouldn't try to leave if I wasn't."

"So who called?"

She didn't answer. But at his determined expression, her lips quivered and tears began to well.

"It...it was *him*," she admitted reluctantly.

"What did he want?" Raven demanded, but in a gentler tone.

"It doesn't matter. I-I just have to get home."

"You're not going anywhere till you tell me." His gaze was kind, concerned but firm, as he pushed her back down.

She glared up at him.

"Tell me," he insisted.

Her eyes grew huge. "He...he said...a little girl smothers easy."

"So why the hell didn't you say that in the first place?" Raven ripped back the rest of her covers.

"No...no reason." But her low tone was quavery.

She was lying—again.

"You've got to call home and warn them while I dress," she said.

"Right." He watched her slide out of bed and begin to undo the strings of her hospital gown. She'd slipped an arm halfway out of a sleeve before she looked up and realized she was undressing in front of him as if they were man and wife, as if such casual intimacies with him were the most natural thing in all the world.

Hot color rose in her cheeks when she saw him observing her with devastating interest. She yanked her gown back on.

"What have you got to be embarrassed about?" he murmured. "It's not as if I haven't seen it all before."

"Well, you're not seeing it again!" she snapped, stepping hurriedly into the bathroom. "And make that call!"

But when he picked up the phone, he couldn't get through.

Dust curled behind the pickup in the early morning light as they roared up to Judith's long limestone ranch house. If only Raven hadn't been so concerned about Innocence's little girl and so aware of her fear, he would have thought the morning lovely because he was free and she was beside him.

There seemed nothing ominous in the bucolic setting. It seemed impossible to imagine that Noah had gotten there before them.

A lone whippoorwill's song broke the morning quiet. Dew clung to the tall grasses. A fiery dawn backlighted the thick towering fringe of dark cypress trees along the creek. But Innocence with her lovely red hair and long white neck was the most beautiful of all.

"Look, I appreciate all you've done," Innocence said jerkily when he stopped.

Then why was she so damned anxious to be rid of him?

"Yes, you're undyingly grateful," he murmured dryly.

"The way you came over last night, the way you saved me and then carried me to the hospital," she went on rather gushingly. "I'll never be able to thank you." She paused. "But...but I really still think it best not to see each other again. I should never have come to Panjo's." She paused. "I should never have slept with you."

"Why did you then?"

"Out of guilt."

"You're sure that was the only reason?"

She looked uncomfortable when his dark intent gaze searched her face.

"Of course." But the words seemed to stick in her throat.

Unable to resist touching her, he lifted aside a molten strand of hair. She jumped wildly away.

"Why did you say you loved me, Innocence?"

"That was just part of the act."

"You were pretty convincing."

"Don't!"

"Hey," he murmured in an easy voice that masked the wretched state of his true feelings. "I understand. I regret my actions, too. My only excuse is I had to be rough the last two years or I never would have survived. It was sort of hard to switch gears." He paused. "But I'm sorry I was so rough on you. I came over last night to make it up to you. And I'm not about to leave today till I'm sure your little girl is safe."

His arms wound around her shoulders as if to mold her to his muscular length, but she pushed him away.

"No! I have to handle this my own way," she said thickly. "You have your life. I have mine."

"Maybe one day we will, but until we stop him, it's not that simple. Noah tried to hurt you because you got me out of prison. I have to protect you."

"No! You don't owe me anything."

"For better or worse, you've got me fighting on your side now."

"Please, Raven, you've done enough."

"What are you so afraid of? I promise you . . . I'll never deliberately hurt you again."

Her breath seemed to stop as she leaned toward him and studied his lean, hard face. "Whatever there once was between us—well, it's over now. This has to be goodbye, Raven. Forever. You have to go and let me take care of Ashley."

Innocence flung open the door, but he caught her wrist before she could run.

She tugged at his hand, but she was no match for his strength. He felt her pulse beating wildly. Her breath seemed to stop.

"What are you so scared of?" he whispered.

"You!"

And realizing she was telling the truth, that she was terrified of him, he let her go.

But his stark gaze followed her as she raced to the guest house. He hoped that she might turn back and wave to him before going inside.

But she didn't.

He felt a profound, soul-numbing emptiness. A terrifying coldness seeped inside him.

What would he do if she couldn't ever forgive him?

Raven sucked in a deep, painful breath and got out of his truck to go after her.

Thirteen

Without bothering to knock, Raven stalked inside the guest house with a heavy scowl on his lean face. Even before he caught the snatches of frightened whispers echoing from the hall, he sensed something somber and frighteningly wrong in the heavy chill of the quiet living room.

"Ashley gone... But where? How could she get out? The doors and windows were all locked. I checked on her not an hour ago."

Raven strode soundlessly down the hall and found Marcie and Innocence huddled over a frothily draped crib. His gaze swept the pink walls, baseboards, windowsills and painted furniture. He saw rose carpet. There were rose organdy ruffles at the windows. More than a dozen pink teddy bears were propped in a row upon a toy chest. The only signs that a real child inhabited the room were the scuffed table in one corner littered with jars full of scrambling bugs and odd-looking rocks and the two mud-spattered hightops and two dirty socks beside them. The room was too cloyingly *decorated,* too perfect and too feminine to suit Raven. *Too Judith.*

Raven stared directly into Innocence's panic-stricken eyes.

"I told you to go," she whispered.

"I'm not much good at taking orders," he murmured.

"Go!"

He stayed where he was, his attention drawn to a framed snapshot on the pink bureau of a little girl petting a black lab puppy.

She had jet curls and green eyes.

"No!" Innocence cried in alarm, springing toward the bureau.

But he was faster. Very slowly he picked up the silver frame and held it high above her head. His green gaze narrowed cynically as he studied the child.

His heart had begun to pound.

Except for the frilly dress, he could have been looking at a baby picture of himself.

The child had his eyes. His unruly black hair.

His smile.

His mind screamed.

This couldn't be happening.

"How old is she?" Raven demanded, letting his arm fall.

She snatched the picture. "Why does it matter?"

"Sixteen months," Marcie replied.

"Please! Just go," Innocence said.

"Not now, honey." Roughly, quickly, he did the mathematical calculation. "She's mine, isn't she?" he said, his hard eyes gleaming with emerald fire as he towered over Innocence.

"Isn't she?" he thundered, cornering her.

Innocence's breath froze. She stood perfectly still, fighting to appear calm although he sensed the jarring tension in her.

He turned to Marcie and spoke quickly, urgently, issuing orders as efficiently as a general in a voice of steel. "Go to the main house. Wake everybody up. Tell them Ashley's gone. Call the sheriff. Get Doug and anybody else he can get to volunteer over here to help search."

When Marcie headed obediently toward the door, Innocence would have followed. But Raven caught her arm and snapped her against the wall. Too late he remembered her injuries from her fall and relaxed his grip.

"Damn you, Innocence Lescuer. How could you keep my child from me?"

"How could I tell you?" she whispered. "You were a stranger. We agreed on one night. You took precautions."

"Obviously not enough."

"I . . . I thought the last thing you would ever want was a child."

"No strings . . ." He smiled bitterly as if the memory wasn't a fond one. There was no trace of gentleness or kindness in his tough chiseled features. His hard arms wrapped her tighter until she cried out again. "One night was your idea. Not mine. And there *are* strings."

"I'm sorry, but like I said, it never occurred to me you would want my child."

"*Our child.* It never occurred to me either, until I found out we had one."

She regarded him with dark, tormented eyes. "*We* both know you hate me."

He felt burningly angry. "Do *we?* How can you be so sure of that, when I'm far from sure about my feelings for you?" He released her abruptly, and raked a weary hand through his black hair. "At the moment I don't feel too friendly. But Ashley's my child, too. Not just yours. My responsibility, too. *Ours.*"

"You were so filled with hate in prison that I couldn't imagine you were capable of the kind of love a parent should have for a child."

His blistering gaze sliced her. "Don't lie. You never planned to tell me. If you had, you would have come back to Landerley and found out I was in a helluva lot of trouble a long time ago. You would have said something yesterday." He paused. "And you couldn't have been more wrong... about me. Maybe I would have preferred to be married to the mother of my child, but I do want Ashley. As much as you want her. And if anything has happened to her, I'll never forgive you."

Innocence drew a shallow breath. "Well, at least that much is true. If anything goes wrong—I am always to blame."

She had gone very white, and suddenly the naked, uncontrollable guilt and terror he saw in her face cut through his own sorrow and black rage.

"I'll never be able to forgive myself, either—a second time," she said in a suffocated whisper.

"What do you mean?" His dark tone was infinitesimally gentler.

"When I was married to Matthew, we had another child. A son—Timmy. When he died Matthew blamed me, and the guilt destroyed our marriage. The whole thing nearly killed me. So, you'll get your revenge if Ashley's been hurt. I don't think I could survive feeling responsible for such a loss a second time."

When Innocence fought to push past him, Raven pulled her gently into his arms. As she struggled to turn her head away from his, her long hair tangled around his hand. He used it as leverage to hold her tightly to him.

"Forgive me," he whispered brokenly, "for being so thoughtlessly cruel to you again." When she hesitated, he stroked her neck and pleaded with her again. "Tell me about your son."

"No!"

"Please—"

She began haltingly. "He was only six, but such a handful. Our house was on a high cliff near the water. And one day he wandered away from Matthew and the babysitter down to the beach. He must have fallen and hit his head on a rock or something. He was pulled from the water unconscious. If I hadn't been at the hospital, if I'd been home... We gave him mouth-to-mouth, oxygen, *everything,* but he died on the operating table."

He felt the pain in her as if it were his own. "It wasn't your fault." Raven gripped her more tightly against himself. "And it's not your fault for Ashley. This is more my fault than yours. Noah hates me. Everything that has happened...my going to prison, the way I treated you, last night in the barn...all of it has been my fault. Not yours. You'll never know how deeply I regret hurting you last night. I'm sorry about the things I said, the things I did...."

"It doesn't matter," she said. "Nothing will ever matter again—not if we don't find Ashley."

"I'll find her. If it's the last thing I do, I'll bring her home safe to you. I swear it."

But even as he swore it, he felt her go tense with fear.

And his heart was filled with a terror even greater than hers.

*   *   *

All through the rest of that long day Raven refused to give up hope, even when the sun completed its arc and began to sink, even when the other searchers quit for supper, even when he was utterly weary and mindlessly retrudging the same ground he'd gone over hours earlier. The Lescuer ranch wasn't that big, but there were dense groves of cedar. There were caves and canyons hollowed into the limestone hills—a thousand places where a small child could get lost or be deliberately hidden.

It had soon been discovered that Ashley's favorite puppy, Blackie, was missing too. Sheriff Orley had checked into Raven's theory about Noah and found out that not only did he have a record for rape and drunken driving, but his latest girlfriend had complained of harassing phone calls and had vanished under mysterious circumstances.

The sheriff had set up roadblocks on all county roads leading to and from the ranch. The police in the surrounding counties were alerted.

Innocence had said Ashley's favorite place was either the barn where the puppies stayed or a shallow pool beneath the dam at the creek. Raven kept returning to the creek; he hated thinking of Ashley toddling near the dam because the water was very deep and fast in the middle.

The sinking sun filled Raven with dread since the search would be called off at night. As he tramped toward the creek, the tall limestone cliffs cast long shadows. He heard the creek and paused, hoping Ashley wasn't terrified and alone, hoping she wouldn't have to spend a night outside.

Hoping she was still alive.

And as he stood there, it seemed to him that he heard the gurgle of childish laughter. Not trusting his ears, he called Ashley's name and then strained to listen.

He heard a joyous bark. A black lab puppy bounded out of the brush.

Raven shouted Ashley's name again, as he knelt to pet the puppy who came up and began clumsily clawing the leg of his jeans.

"You must be Blackie. Where is she, fella?" A terrible fear began to mount in Raven.

But as he stroked the black fur, Raven saw a tentative movement near the fringe of trees.

Blackie barked. Raven caught his breath as an exquisite miniature replica of himself stepped coyly out from the line of trees.

Her black curls were tangled. Her pink lace nightgown was torn and muddy. Her diaper appeared sodden.

Not that she cared. She seemed to be in her own world. Her dark head bent as if she were inspecting with vague interest something she held in her left hand.

"Ashley!"

Giving him a long, curious look, she began to suck her thumb worriedly. Then she began backing toward the trees.

Raven sank lower on his knees, so he wouldn't look so tall and she could get used to him. "Ashley?" he called in a softer tone. "I won't hurt you. See—Blackie's not scared of me."

She stopped and hid her head shyly. "Mama?"

"Honey, your mama's not feeling well and she's back at the house. I promised her I'd find you for her. Do you want me to take you home—to her?"

Ashley peeped up at him with her big, bashful eyes.

His eyes.

"Do you want your Mama, Ashley?"

"Mama." She nodded and walked toward him very slowly.

Raven stayed very still when she placed a timid hand beside his on the dog.

"Bwackie," she said.

"Where have you been all day?" Raven asked gently.

She yawned and a vague, troubled look passed across her features. "Man—bad." Then she rubbed her eyes sleepily. "See!" She held out her clenched hand and peeled back one small finger at a time.

Three deadly .38-caliber bullets glowed in her tiny innocent palm.

Noah had shot Pam with a .38. Three times.

At the sight of the bullets, Raven felt savage loathing. And terror.

Black all-engulfing terror.

The child slyly closed her hand again.

"Where did you get those, sweetheart?"

"Mine." She hid her treasure behind her back and began to suck her thumb. "Ridin.'"

With cool, calculating eyes, Raven scanned the tall cliffs, the lonely trees, the vast brown stretch of empty meadow. The bastard had taken her away in his car. He could have done anything to her. He'd brought her back and left her at the creek—where anything could have happened to her. She could have fallen into the cold, deep water so easily.

A chill went through Raven. "How would you like to hear a story about a white wolf on the way home?"

"Are wolfs nice?"

"This one will be."

Raven surveyed the desolate landscape again. Even now Noah could be anywhere—somewhere near, above them on the cliffs, behind a boulder or the trees, inside a crevice—watching them. He could be drawing deadly aim with a high-powered rifle.

Or he could be miles away.

As Raven lifted the precious little girl into his arms and hurriedly strode back to the house, he felt the same all-consuming fear he'd known in prison when he'd realized Snake was determined to kill him and would fight to the death.

Noah wasn't going to quit, either.

The brilliantly lit house stood out against the purple sky as Raven dragged himself wearily toward it with the sleeping Ashley clutched tightly in his arms. The black lab puppy whose paws were full of burrs limped pitifully behind them.

When Raven reached the fenced yard, Blackie sat down, held up a paw and whined. Raven heard a terrified scream from the lighted porch. Black Dog yelped and bounded out to lick her pup and greet them. Then there was a smothered little disbelieving cry of joy.

"Matthew, look—"

A slim woman with flame dark hair and a white silk dress unfolded herself from the arms of a large blond man and came flying down the steps toward him. The porch light backlighted her slender form and set her red hair on fire.

"Ashley—is she all right?" Innocence began almost fearfully.

"She's sleeping," Raven reassured her gently.

Ashley lifted her head groggily. "No, I not sleep! Mama!"

But when Innocence held out her arms the child laid her head once more on the broad shoulder of the tall, dark man who'd carried her all the way from the creek and clung to him.

Raven felt the need to defend Ashley's refusal to go to her. "I told her a story on the way back and she fell asleep," Raven said. "I didn't know I was such a story-teller."

"Good stowy," Ashley murmured, defending him. "About dogs and nice wolfs."

"She's never taken to a stranger so quickly before."

Those words and Innocence's soft smile of wonder filled him with a poignant fatherly pride as he followed her inside, carrying their drowsy child through the crowded living room, which was jammed with family, neighbors and county law officers. Ashley smiled sleepily at all of them even though she refused to relinquish her grip on Raven neck's, stubbornly clutching him tighter even when her aunt and her grandmother begged her to come to them.

Raven stayed with Innocence while she fed Ashley and then bathed her and put her into clean, dry clothes and her pink crib. Raven reveled in the miraculous sweetness he found in these everyday activities between mother and child. The fact that they included him as if he belonged, made his anger toward Innocence for not telling him about Ashley lessen.

Ashley grabbed her brush, stood up, stomping her feet when her mother pulled it through her tangled hair, demanding that Raven do it instead.

"She has certainly taken to you," Innocence said.

And as Ashley sat obediently while he ever so gently ran the brush through the snarls in her hair, he felt a special happiness he had never known before.

He even laughed when she childishly took the brush from him, stood up in her crib like a little empress, demanding, as if he were now hers to command, that he fetch every single one of her pink teddy bears because she said she was afraid to sleep alone after the "bad man."

They could get nothing more than that phrase out of her.

"If Noah hurt her," Innocence began, when Raven finished telling Ashley a story about another magic white wolf who was really a prince and the child had fallen asleep, "I'll never, never forgive myself...."

Raven threaded his fingers in hers after she had finished tucking the coverlet around their daughter and pulled her close. "You're too hard on yourself."

"Can you ever forgive me, Raven?" she pleaded.

"I already have." His voice was soft.

He remembered his own loveless childhood, his mother who'd cared more for her glamourous career and wealthy friends than she had for him. Innocence was so sweet and loving with Ashley.

"You've done a wonderful job with Ashley. I'll be grateful to you for that forever." Raven's emerald eyes locked with hers. "Noah didn't hurt her. She's fine. But tomorrow I want you to leave and take her back to San Francisco with you."

"You're sending us away?"

"So you'll be safe."

"What about Noah?"

"It's me he wants."

On a shudder she clasped his hard hand more tightly. "You were wonderful to search for her so long after everyone else had given up for the day, wonderful now to want to protect us—"

He was basking in her praise, hanging on to her next words, hoping...when suddenly a deep masculine voice from behind them shattered the intimate mood.

"There you are," Matthew said.

Innocence smiled when she saw the great golden bear of a man filling the doorway behind them.

"Yes?" she whispered.

"Judith sent me to check and see what's taking you two so long."

"We're through," Innocence murmured. "I was just thanking Raven."

"You have my thanks as well, White," Matthew said generously.

Matthew was handsome and elegantly dressed in a three-piece suit that might look right in San Francisco but was too much for Landerley. Still, there seemed something so very safe about his smooth, placid face. Raven's stomach knotted. Matthew looked like a stockbroker or a banker—someone who spent his life quietly, passionlessly pushing papers behind a desk.

Innocence had been married to this man, borne her first beloved child by him. She'd been dating him, and now she probably wanted to remarry him. Matthew would be Ashley's father.

A cold, hard core of empty nothingness seemed to expand inside Raven as he backed out of the light, away from them.

"Raven," Innocence whispered and then choked on a sob.

"Goodbye," he said quietly.

"Goodbye." Innocence's tear-filled gaze seemed suddenly to burn holes in Raven's ravaged face. She swayed toward him. Raven realized she had looked at him like that once before, when she'd lain in his arms and said she was memorizing him.

Raven's dark gaze was equally intense.

Not that he would ever be able to forget her.

I love her, Raven thought dully, aware of a strange cold band of pain imprisoning his heart.

I've always loved her.

But he had to let her go. This man could offer her more than he could. At least she would be safe with Matthew.

Still, the thought of losing her tore Raven to pieces. Unable to bear it, Raven pivoted abruptly and stalked past her into the hall. She called after him, but that only made him run faster.

Vaguely he was aware of Judith smiling triumphantly as Innocence cried after him again. He rushed blindly out into the all-enveloping dark and tore across the open meadow.

Even though he was too numb to feel the pain, he knew the fierce anguish would come later.

Without Innocence, the rest of his life would loom before him as hellishly as the most terrible prison sentence.

He would always love her.

But that was why he had to let her go.

Fourteen

Something had broken in Innocence when Raven looked at her with such mute desperation, his handsome face wooden and white with pain, his burning eyes dark and wild before he'd fled.

The minute he was gone a painful knot of misery congealed in her throat and she would have flung herself had not her mother thrust herself in her path. All Innocence could do was call Raven's name.

Not that he heeded that strangled, helpless cry that even to her own ears sounded far away, surreal.

"Let him go," Judith said. "It's for the best. He's not your kind. Or Ashley's. He...he hardly seems tame."

She had told herself the same thing—that Raven was so dark and wild all he could ever feel for her was the need to take and punish.

"Mother, I told you I'm not going back to Matthew. Matthew understands. Why can't you?"

"I do understand—that," Judith agreed slowly as she went to Ashley's crib and possessively inspected her sleeping granddaughter. Judith's face glowed now that everything was turning out as she wanted. "But that doesn't mean you should resume your relationship with *that* odious man again. If you really love Ashley—"

Innocence joined her mother at the crib, and as Innocence looked down at her sleeping child, she couldn't resist touching her glossy black curls.

Ashley was so much like Raven. Innocence realized that even if she didn't love Raven, she would never again be able to look at or touch Ashley without wanting Raven there, too. He had missed so much—his mother's love, the last two years of his life. How could she let him walk out of her life? How could she pretend that Raven didn't matter?

When he mattered more than anything.

Ashley had been drawn to him, too, as she'd never been drawn to another. Innocence smiled when she thought of how gentle he'd been with his little girl. How protective. If he were evil as her mother said, how could Ashley be so adorable—when she was so much like him?

"Raven White is a monster," Judith said.

Her mother had always run her down, too.

"No, he's Ashley's father."

"He doesn't have to be. You will meet some new man. You can still marry—"

Innocence's hands clenched the guardrail to the crib. "No!"

"Your worst trait is that you never listen to me!"

"Do you think you'll ever be able to accept the fact that I have to live my own life . . . even if it doesn't please you? That I can't be another Linda?"

"Why do you act like I'm so unreasonable? All I've ever wanted was your happiness," Judith said rather melodramatically.

"No, all you've ever wanted is what you wanted. My dreams have never been yours."

"Why are we having this ridiculous conversation when you can go back to California, when you can go home and pretend none of this ever happened?"

"Home... Isn't there some trite expression that home is where one's heart is?"

"Don't do this! He's a hard, impossible man! He used you!"

Innocence turned away from her mother and the crib. Innocence would never be able to understand her mother any more than her mother would be able to understand her.

Was Raven really so awful?

If he was hard, hadn't his life made him hard?

If he was hard, why had he come the minute he'd thought she was in danger? Why had he fought for her at the risk of his own life?

Hadn't he stood up to Judith as she herself had always longed to do? Wasn't that the real reason that Judith, who loved to bully people, hated him?

Innocence remembered how Ashley had clung to Raven and ordered him about as if she sensed her claim on him, how he had searched for her tirelessly and been infinitely gentle when he had found her. When they had fed and bathed the child together, it had seemed that for that short space of time they had been a real family.

Raven had forgiven her for not telling him about Ashley.

And in that darkest hour when they had both feared Ashley might be lost to them forever, Raven had not blamed her. He had comforted her.

Raven wanted to know his child.

So, why had he walked out like that when Matthew had come in?

Because he must have drawn the conclusion that she wanted Matthew. Because when she had told Matthew that she loved Raven, Raven had been away looking for Ashley.

The wondrous thought came to her that Raven wasn't hard and selfish. He was selfless. Even though he had wanted her and his child, he was willing to send them away because his first priorities were their safety and happiness. Above his own happiness, he put theirs.

He would even allow Innocence to leave him for another man.

Her mother was wrong. Wrong. Wrong.

His actions were not those of a selfish, hard man.

Sadness welled up inside Innocence at the thought of him thinking she might want to marry anyone other than him when her life would be empty without him.

He was everything.

Everyone else in her life, though dear to her in their way, would never be enough. Not even Ashley would be enough.

If you really love your daughter...

Her mother's words.

When had her mother ever known what she needed to be happy?

I do love my daughter.

But I love Raven, too.

If I really loved Ashley, wouldn't I at least try to work out a relationship with her father?

Tears streamed silently down Innocence's cheeks as she turned to Matthew and said very softly, "Thank you for understanding. I only wish my mother..."

Her mother's face twisted, and her veined hand moved toward her heart.

"Don't even think about faking an attack, Mother," Innocence said. "I can't let myself be manipulated or made to feel guilty for making this decision. Raven is Ashley's father. And I love him."

"Quit saying that!" Judith said shrilly.

"It's the truth, Mother. And I've got to go to him and see if he'll have me. And I don't care what any of you think."

"This is the most outrageous thing you've ever done!"

"Please try to be happy for me, Mother," Innocence whispered. "He's not the man you say he is. He never was. You did him a grievous wrong when you kept silent and let him go to prison. Someday soon I hope you'll go to him and beg his forgiveness. And I promise you that he will forgive you. As I will forgive you."

Then Innocence was running away.

Out of her mother's house.

Into the purple darkness.

To find the only man she would always love.

Because of her injuries, Innocence had to pace herself to make the long walk through the high grasses and across the creek bottom. Thus, she was many minutes behind Raven when she crossed the slippery dam and found herself utterly alone beneath the tall, dark cypress trees. Moonlight sifted through the thin leaves and shimmered faintly on the flowing waters.

She thought the dark woods and the silvery water beautiful until a twig snapped behind her.

Then she knew again the terrible fear she had known in the barn. Adrenaline pumped through her in icy shock waves as she began to run faster. So fast that she was gasping for breath and aching all over when she reached Raven's darkened house.

She stopped in the blackest shadows near the porch and called his name.

He didn't answer.

The eerie silence unnerved her. The house seemed desolate in the moonlight, remote and lonely—like the man.

The wind sighed in the trees, and she felt an uneasy trickle of awareness go through her. What if he wasn't here? What if Noah had followed her again?

She heard something behind her. Terrified, she ran to the back of the house.

That was when she saw the single light burning in Raven's tool shed.

Then she knew he was home.

She was safe.

The door to the toolshed was slightly ajar and Innocence stopped, clinging to the shadowy darkness so she could study him for a long moment.

A naked light bulb made a bright halo above his black head. He had discarded his shirt and was working bare chested, and she noted the ripple of hard muscles across his shoulders and down his pale arms every time he lifted a fence post and stacked it in the pile beside a roll of barbed wire and boxes of fence staples, which were neatly arranged by the door. An ax and a chain saw had been moved to the door of the shed as well.

He looked tired, weary of life itself. There were gray smudges of exhaustion under his beautiful eyes; his olive-toned skin was a sickly white; he was still too thin from prison. Yet to her he was more breathtakingly handsome than any other man alive.

Because she loved him.

"Raven—"

At that breathy sound, he started, his tired eyes straining to penetrate the darkness.

"It's just me," she whispered.

"Just you?"

When he saw her, the post he'd been holding fell abruptly. He just stood there, his gaze fierce and bitterly forbidding.

"Innocence?"

She clung to the shadows like a wild creature afraid to come into the light. Her hair tumbled over her shoulders; her voice had been breathy, unrecognizable because of her long walk. Her jeans and shoes were soaked and muddy from crossing the creek bottom.

"Yes," she said, stepping hesitantly up the steps toward him. "It's me."

"What the hell are you doing here?" he rasped in a low, tortured tone. "I thought you wanted Matthew..."

"No." Keeping her eyes fastened on the stack of posts beside him, she said in a small voice, "I-I had to talk to you."

"Not tonight." He grabbed his shirt and began pulling it on. "I'll drive you back."

"No! I can't ever go...home again. Not after I told Mother I was coming here."

Raven's eyes blazed. "You have to go back. Matthew—"

"I'm not going back with Matthew. I told him that while you were out looking for Ashley."

"What?" There was a bitter tension in Raven's hard face. But he was too stunned to do or say anything more for a long moment. "Why not?" he finally managed in an odd voice.

Her knees felt rubbery and weak. He seemed so harsh, so cold. How could she find the courage to say what was in her heart? "Because I don't love him. Because all I-I want ... all I've ever wanted since I met you ... was to be with you," she whispered. "You asked me to move in with you."

"That was before—"

"Well, I will ... move in. I want to."

"Are you crazy?"

She interrupted him before he could finish. "I-I know from what you said that you couldn't ever love me, that you wouldn't ever want marriage—" Her mouth trembled. Tears beaded her lashes. She felt like an idiot. She couldn't say anything more.

Raven stared at her mute, tortured face for a long baffled moment. Slowly the truth that she had chosen him sank in.

She wanted him.

Then with shocking speed and surprising agility he moved toward her, gathering her tightly in his arms. "You little fool," he muttered softly. "Is that what you think?"

"All I know is that I could never go back to San Francisco ... without you," she murmured in a choked voice against his warm shoulder.

Suddenly she was too shy, too nervous, and embarrassed to go on. "This is so hard," she said. "Even harder than hitching that ride with you that first day."

"Try," he said. "You were good that day."

"I want to be with you ... for as long as you'll have me, Raven White."

"Wyatt," he whispered. "Raven Wyatt."

Not that she heard him.

"Innocence," he groaned from deep within his chest, crushing her to him. "Oh, Innocence." Then he caught her face between his large capable hands and kissed her passionately. "I can't give you what Matthew can. At least not for a while."

"You can give me all I'll ever need."

"It's too dangerous for you to be here with me," Raven murmured.

"But can I stay?"

"Forever, my darling," he whispered as he lifted her into his strong arms and carried her toward the house.

Inside the house he held her gently, his arms wrapped around her as he savored the wonder of her coming to him. His lips caressed hers with velvet-soft kisses as if she were infinitely precious to him. He was tender, but his tenderness contained a passionate depth of emotion that made her tremble.

"Will you marry me?" he asked, his voice warm and deep.

"What?"

His breath was hot against her skin. "I don't want to make love to you again without knowing you'll be my wife."

"You don't have to marry me because of Ashley. I don't expect—"

"It's because of you, my darling. Only because of you. I love you. If you hadn't run off that first night, I would have asked you to marry me then."

She blushed hoping he would say more. When he didn't, she laughed softly. "I love you too."

Their gazes melted together. His thumbs raked across her lips. Then he cupped her face in his hands and tilted it back into the silvery light, staring at her in wonder. He had lived in darkness so long, he had never thought he could feel so gloriously alive and filled with hope. He felt his bitterness sliding away, and as he lost himself in her beautiful brown eyes he felt a sweetness he had never known.

They were clinging, kissing gently, joyously when a hate-filled voice hissed from the shadows.

"How very touching."

The lovers jerked apart.

Innocence went numb with shock.

"Noah," Raven said harshly.

A dark figure stepped toward them. Moonlight glinted off the barrel of his gun, off his smiling white teeth. "You took Pam. I want Innocence."

"Let her go. Take me. It's me you hate," Raven said, his voice very slow and deliberate.

"That's why it's her I'll kill. That's why I'll let you live. The way I did before."

"You bastard!"

Noah's face was devoid of all emotion save grim satisfaction as he reached for Innocence.

But when he would have yanked her brutally away from Raven, a killing rage misted in Raven's eyes.

Snake and his three thugs had come at him with that hand-tooled shank.

Fight or die.

That had been the rule in *C* block.

That was the rule now.

Maybe prison had hardened him, but it had also taught him to fight—to the death if necessary.

This bastard had killed Pam and condemned him to the hell of prison. This savage had kidnapped Ashley.

Noah's left hand closed around Innocence's shoulder.

With a violent cry, Raven lunged straight at the other hand—the one that held the gun.

One minute Noah's fingers were digging into Innocence's arm; in the next she was free.

Noah yelped once in sudden terror and surprise. Then he pulled the trigger as Raven lunged and knocked him to the ground.

The bullets went wild. Then the two men were grappling on the hard wooden floor, heaving each other against the furniture.

A chair crashed to the ground. A lamp shattered. Broken bits of glass cut into Raven's arm.

Noah was larger. He tried to cling tenaciously to the gun. But Raven got on top of him and pinned him to the floor, his fist pounding into his fleshy face with such violence that the gun finally fell.

Innocence crawled quickly across the floor and grabbed it. It was still warm and sweaty from Noah's hand, and she was so revolted she screamed as she tossed it out the window.

Raven kept pounding Noah against the floor. Even when Noah no longer had the strength to fight back, Raven hit him relentlessly. When Noah's head lolled back and he collapsed unconscious, Raven's large hands dug crushingly into his throat.

"Don't kill him," Innocence whispered from behind him, terrified not of Noah now but for Raven. "Please don't kill him. You'll hate yourself forever if you do."

Raven heard her through the killing mist. *Let him go? Was she crazy?*

"Raven, don't . . . don't let him turn you into a killer, too."

Slowly her soft, pleading voice penetrated Raven's consciousness. With a savage jerk he released Noah's throat and let the unconscious man fall to the floor. He hadn't killed Snake, either, when he'd had Snake's knife. When he'd dropped it, Arredo had grabbed it and stabbed Snake. Not that anyone had believed Raven.

"Call Orley," Raven whispered as he stood up, breathing hard, his wild eyes burning fiercely as he gulped in air.

More than anything in the world he wanted to finish Noah. As he had wanted to finish Snake.

Raven's lust for violence warred with some other gentler need as it had that other time.

"It's over," Innocence said gently after she'd made the call to the police, putting her arms around Raven and dabbing at the thin trickle of blood that ran from his split lip to his chin. "It's finally over."

He saw the tears glittering in her eyes.

And her touch, her love banished the violence.

Slowly Raven nodded and pulled her into his arms and touched her lovely face with his bruised hands while she clung to him trustingly. He did not want to disappoint her or hurt her ever again. And slowly all the anger and hate in his heart was replaced by the sweetness of the woman in his arms.

She was his—forever.

From this moment forward love would reign supreme in his heart.

"No," he whispered, "our real lives are just beginning.

Then he bent his head and kissed her. Very tenderly.

"I love you," he whispered, his eyes gleaming with green fire. With her in his arms, it seemed wonderful to face the future. With her in his arms, he suddenly realized he could face his past, too.

He wanted to see his sister, his father, even Astella. The pain of the past was gone forever because he had a future with this woman.

But tomorrow would be soon enough to tell Innocence about his family, to tell her who he really was, that his name wasn't really White—but Wyatt, to tell her that San Francisco had once been his home, too.

And would be again.

At last he had everything he had always wanted.

Raven's fingers curled around hers as he led her out of the darkness into the silvery moonlight and crushed her tightly to himself. And as always her tantalizing kiss was both innocent and wild.

"My darling. My sweet hitchhiker," he murmured.

And he said it so sweetly, she did not mind.

Epilogue

———

Raven Wyatt was a happy man. He had found love. And
he had come home.

Outside the Wyatt mansion in Pacific Heights, the San
Francisco twilight was soft and fragrant with the scent of
jasmine. Bright stars were popping out in a darkening in-
digo sky.

Inside the house, rock music vibrated through the vast
rooms that magic spring evening. Honey's step-son,
Mario, was pounding his drums with a vengeance. Not that
anybody minded enough to complain. The chaotic music
was perfect for the cheerful chaos of Ashley Wyatt's third
birthday party.

Hunter Wyatt's former house, which had once been as
perfect and well ordered as a movie set, was now filled with
a hodgepodge of furnishings and small racing children,
their parents and their grandparents. There were numer-

ous babies in attendance, too—one of them being Raven's
own redheaded baby son, Stuart.

Raven's brother-in-law, Joshua, and his lawyer, Johnny
Midnight, were there with their beautiful wives and children. Midnight and Joshua had become Raven's business
partners and his best friends, the three having bonded almost instantly after Raven had returned to San Francisco
to make his peace with his father.

Raven had found it easy to forgive Hunter Wyatt who
was a frail shadow of his former overbearing self. Hunter
admitted he'd had regrets of his own and had tried to find
Raven. Though still lovely, Astella was older and content
with her marriage. They had been only too happy to accept Raven and to retire and leave their businesses in his
capable hands and those of his sister, Honey. Honey loved
working with her long lost brother as much he liked
working with her, and every day they grew closer. She had
confided in him that she had missed him for years. He had
told her that he had intended to visit her before he was accused of murder and that right before he'd gone to prison
he'd sent her a painting of them as children so that at least
she'd know he was still alive.

From the landing, Raven grinned when his eye caught
his wife's and then his sister's. Honey was wearing the
most atrocious green flowered dress. Her children were
dressed in green too. Even Joshua had a green tie.

Innocence was twirling a blindfolded Ashley in front of
a cardboard donkey. Ashley was so excited she dropped
the tail twice and Honey had to pick it up when she
creamed, and put it in her small hand again.

The drums rolled as Ashley stumbled forward and,
missing the proper spot, pinned the tail to the donkey's
eye. When everybody laughed at her, the little girl tore off
her blindfold and wept with bitter disappointment. She

ripped the tail out of the eye and threw it on the floor
Then she grabbed the donkey poster and yanked it in two
before racing up the stairs to her daddy.

Raven lifted her high into his arms and hugged her small
sobbing body until she quieted. As he descended the stair
with his precious, although very spoiled daughter wrapped
in his arms, he felt like a king who had everything in life he
could ever want. Prison seemed a lifetime behind him now
that he had known the joys of a harmonious marriage with
the one woman he truly loved. Now that he had come
home and made peace with his father. Now that he him
self was a proud father of two children he adored.

Now he found only pride and happiness in this beauti
ful room with the tall windows, where he'd once hidden
behind huge canvasses and sadly longed for his mother to
love him.

Innocence picked up Stuart and came to him. Smiling up
at Raven she whispered, "He's having the time of his life."

"So am I," Raven said, admiring his wife and his chil
dren, admiring the grand house that finally felt like a
home. "I have everything I could ever want. I—"

The doorbell rang and interrupted him.

A dozen children scrambled to answer it.

When it was thrown open, Judith Lescuer stepped un
certainly inside. She hadn't attended the wedding. Nor
Ashley's second birthday party. Nor Stuart's christening

"She's wearing black," Raven murmured.

"But she came," Innocence said, pressing his hand ea
gerly, she whispered, her eyes shining, "Now be good."

Judith came up to them. She eyed her grandson and In
nocence and then said querulously, "He has red hair like
my father. He has long fingers . . . like I do."

Raven held out his hand to his mother-in-law. "We're
glad you came, Judith. You can hold him . . . if you like."

Judith lifted the baby from her daughter's arms. "It was high time—that I came. He's adorable."

Judith's eyes met Raven's. A single tear hung suspended from her thin gray lashes. She started to speak, but her mouth seemed unable to form the words.

And suddenly he didn't care if she was too proud to beg his forgiveness. He felt the need in her tired old heart, just as she seemed to feel the forgiveness in his.

She sighed. And so did he.

They looked away and waited for the awkward moment to pass.

Someday maybe they would both be able to say the words.

Ashley struggled to get down and go to her grandmother too. Soon the old lady and her two grandchildren were settled on a couch away from the mainstream of the wild festivities, and Ashley was ripping into a birthday present Judith had brought her.

Gently, without speaking, Raven took Innocence in his arms, and his mouth claimed hers in a long, deep kiss.

He wanted more children. He wanted a long life.

But what he wanted most of all was Innocence by his side—forever. He loved her. And she loved him.

"Innocence," Raven murmured her name in an aching murmur against her lips. "You never told me why they call you that."

"Because when I was a little girl I was so bad and wild. And yet every time my parents caught me in some mischief, I always acted innocent."

"Wild Innocence," he whispered on smile. "That fits you. Especially in bed."

She smiled, too. "I love you," she said before his mouth came down again to hungrily possess her lips again.

"I know."

"I hope that doesn't mean you're about to start taking me for granted."

"Never—my love. My darling," he said.

The drums rolled and Mario played his own rendition of their favorite song, "Wildness," while their kiss went on and on.

*   *   *   *   *

SILHOUETTE®

Desire®

They're the hottest books around...

With heroes you've grown to know—and *love*...

Created by Top authors—the ones *you* say are your favorites...

MAN OF THE MONTH: 1994

Don't miss a single one of these handsome hunks—

In January
Secret Agent Man
by *Diana Palmer*

In February
Wild Innocence
by *Ann Major*

In March
Wrangler's Lady
by *Jackie Merritt*

In April
Bewitched
by *Jennifer Greene*

In May
Lucy and the Stone
by *Dixie Browning*

In June
Haven's Call
by *Robin Elliott*

And that's just the first six months! Later in the year, look for books by Joan Hohl, Barbara Boswell, Cait London and Annette Broadrick.

Man of the Month...only from Silhouette Desire

MOM94JJ

Relive the romance...
Harlequin and Silhouette
are proud to present

A program of collections of three complete novels by the most requested
authors with the most requested themes. Be sure to look for one volume each
month with three complete novels by top name authors.

In January: **WESTERN LOVING** Susan Fox
JoAnn Ross
Barbara Kaye

Loving a cowboy is easy—taming him isn't!

In February: **LOVER, COME BACK!** Diana Palmer
Lisa Jackson
Patricia Gardner Evans

It was over so long ago—yet now they're calling, "Lover, Come Back!"

In March: **TEMPERATURE RISING** JoAnn Ross
Tess Gerritsen
Jacqueline Diamond

Falling in love—just what the doctor ordered!

Available at your favorite retail outlet.

REQ-G3

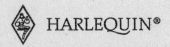 

JOAN JOHNSTON'S

SERIES CONTINUES!

Available in March, *The Cowboy Takes a Wife* (D #842) is the latest addition to Joan Johnston's sexy series about the lives and loves of the irresistible Whitelaw family. Set on a Wyoming ranch, this heart-wrenching story tells the tale of a single mother who desperately needs a husband—a very *big* husband—fast!

Don't miss *The Cowboy Takes a Wife* by Joan Johnston, only from Silhouette Desire.

If you are looking for more titles by

ANN MAJOR

Don't miss this chance to order additional stories by one of Silhouette's most popular authors:

Silhouette Desire®

#05648	THE GOODBYE CHILD	$2.75	☐
#05690	A KNIGHT IN TARNISHED ARMOR	$2.79	☐
#05716	MARRIED TO THE ENEMY	$2.89	☐
#05819	WILD MIDNIGHT	$2.99	☐

Men Made In America

#45159	DREAM COME TRUE	$3.59	☐

Silhouette® Books

#20094	BAD BOYS	$5.50	☐

(By Request series—a 3-in-1 volume containing complete novels by Ann Major, Dixie Browning and Ginna Gray)
(limited quantities available on certain titles)

TOTAL AMOUNT	$
POSTAGE & HANDLING	$
($1.00 for one book, 50¢ for each additional)	
APPLICABLE TAXES*	$ _____
TOTAL PAYABLE	$ _____
(check or money order—please do not send cash)	

To order, complete this form and send it, along with a check or money order for the total above, payable to Silhouette Books, to: *In the U.S.*: 3010 Walden Avenue, P.O. Box 9077, Buffalo, NY 14269-9077; *In Canada*: P.O. Box 636, Fort Erie, Ontario, L2A 5X3.

Name: _____

Address: _____ City: _____

State/Prov.: _____ Zip/Postal Code: _____

*New York residents remit applicable sales taxes.
Canadian residents remit applicable GST and provincial taxes.

AMBACK3

Silhouette®

SILHOUETTE®

Desire®

**COMING IN
FEBRUARY FROM
SILHOUETTE DESIRE...**

**SIX SINGLE GUYS GET A
BIG SURPRISE WHEN THEY FALL HARD
FOR THEIR MS. RIGHT!**

Bachelor Boys

WILD INNOCENCE a *Man of the Month* by Ann Major
YESTERDAY'S OUTLAW by Raye Morgan
SEVEN YEAR ITCH by Peggy Moreland
TWILIGHT MAN by Karen Leabo
RICH GIRL, BAD BOY by Audra Adams
BLACK LACE AND LINEN by Susan Carroll

*THESE SIX SEXY BACHELORS WON'T
KNOW WHAT HITS THEM TILL
THE RING IS ON THEIR FINGER!*

SILHOUETTE... Where Passion Lives

Don't miss these Silhouette favorites by some of our most
distinguished authors! And now you can receive a discount by
ordering two or more titles!

SD	#05772	FOUND FATHER by Justine Davis	$2.89 ☐
SD	#05783	DEVIL OR ANGEL by Audra Adams	$2.89 ☐
SD	#05786	QUICKSAND by Jennifer Greene	$2.89 ☐
SD	#05796	CAMERON by Beverly Barton	$2.99 ☐
IM	#07481	FIREBRAND by Paula Detmer Riggs	$3.39 ☐
IM	#07502	CLOUD MAN by Barbara Faith	$3.50 ☐
IM	#07505	HELL ON WHEELS by Naomi Horton	$3.50 ☐
IM	#07512	SWEET ANNIE'S PASS by Marilyn Pappano	$3.50 ☐
SE	#09791	THE CAT THAT LIVED ON PARK AVENUE by Tracy Sinclair	$3.39 ☐
SE	#09793	FULL OF GRACE by Ginna Ferris	$3.39 ☐
SE	#09822	WHEN SOMEBODY WANTS by Trisha Alexander	$3.50 ☐
SE	#09841	ON HER OWN by Pat Warren	$3.50 ☐
SR	#08866	PALACE CITY PRINCE by Arlene James	$2.69 ☐
SR	#08916	UNCLE DADDY by Kasey Michaels	$2.69 ☐
SR	#08948	MORE THAN YOU KNOW by Phyllis Halldorson	$2.75 ☐
SR	#08954	HERO IN DISGUISE by Stella Bagwell	$2.75 ☐
SS	#27006	NIGHT MIST by Helen R. Myers	$3.50 ☐
SS	#27010	IMMINENT THUNDER by Rachel Lee	$3.50 ☐
SS	#27015	FOOTSTEPS IN THE NIGHT by Lee Karr	$3.50 ☐
SS	#27020	DREAM A DEADLY DREAM by Allie Harrison	$3.50 ☐

(limited quantities available on certain titles)

	AMOUNT	$
DEDUCT:	10% DISCOUNT FOR 2+ BOOKS	$
	POSTAGE & HANDLING	$_____
	($1.00 for one book, 50¢ for each additional)	
	APPLICABLE TAXES*	$_____
	TOTAL PAYABLE	$_____
	(check or money order—please do not send cash)	

To order, complete this form and send it, along with a check or money order
for the total above, payable to Silhouette Books, to: **In the U.S.:** 3010 Walden
Avenue, P.O. Box 9077, Buffalo, NY 14269-9077; **In Canada:** P.O. Box 636,
Fort Erie, Ontario, L2A 5X3.

Name: _____

Address: _____ City: _____

State/Prov.: _____ Zip/Postal Code: _____

*New York residents remit applicable sales taxes.
Canadian residents remit applicable GST and provincial taxes.   SBACK-JM

ᐯ Silhouette®
™